PRAISE FOR

"*Clade* is a brilliant, unsettling and timely novel: a true text of the Anthr[opocene]
in its subtle shuttlings between lives, epochs and eras, and its knitting tog[ether]
the planet's places. Like Barbara Kingsolver's *Flight Behaviour*, its great subj[ect is]
deep time, swift change, and the eeriness of everyday life. Reading *Clade*
leaves us, in Timothy Morton's phrase, 'strange strangers' to ourselves; and makes the Earth seem
an odder, older, more vulnerable home."
Robert Macfarlane, author of *The Old Ways*

"A beautifully written meditation on climate collapse, concentrating on three
generations of an Australian family. Bradley skilfully evokes the particularity of lived
experience, and the novel is full of vivid little moments, although its real triumph
is in setting these in their larger context: a world wrecked by storms and floods,
changes in vegetation and the collapse of bird and bee populations… Bradley's short,
intense novel is as much a hymn to hope as it is a warning." *New Scientist*

"[An] elegantly bleak vision of a climate-change future… urgent, powerful stuff."
The Guardian

"[A]mong the most literate and humane contributions to that slowly emerging
tradition of what is sometimes called 'slow apocalypse' fiction… a near-epic of loss,
remembrance, and steadily diminishing hope." *Locus*

"A lyrical, strangely uplifting book that will stay with you long after you've turned
the final page." Gareth L. Powell, author of *Ack Ack Macaque*

"[T]here is no one like [Bradley] in the imagining of the imminent end time of the
way we live now." *Sydney Review of Books*

"That rarest of novels: one that stares down its harrowing beginning to find a sense
of peace and even of wonder, while being true to itself. All the way through, the
prose is achingly beautiful. Bradley's a magnificent writer and it's all on display here:
sentences and images float, poetic and sharp as crystal." *The Saturday Paper*

"This is the unstinting dreaming and devoted craft-work of a deeply serious,
marvelously accomplished artist taking on the absolutely essential."
Thomas Farber, author of *The Beholder*

"What is really important in this novel is not these brilliantly rendered future
disaster scenarios, but the way epic events are juxtaposed with very human stories…
There is a beauty in the way Bradley depicts sadness with such truthfulness and
honesty. And in very important ways *Clade* is, in fact, a hopeful novel. It is a book
that depicts human life and love as a shining star in the great dark abyss of time…
Clade is not a novel about what is lost, but what we can never lose." SFFWorld

"A melodic, in[...]   [...]*ald Sun*

CLADE

JAMES
BRADLEY

TITAN BOOKS

Clade

Print edition ISBN: 9781785654145

E-book edition ISBN: 9781785655487

Published by Titan Books

A division of Titan Publishing Group Ltd.

144 Southwark Street, London SE1 0UP

www.titanbooks.com

First Titan edition: September 2017

10 9 8 7 6 5 4 3 2 1

Cover design by Adam Laszczuk © Penguin Group (Australia)

Cover photographs; Bees: Deyan Georgiev/500px; Hive: Getty Images

This is a work of fiction. All of the characters, organizations, and events portrayed in this novel are either products of the author's imagination or are used fictitiously.

A CIP catalogue record for this title is available from the British Library.

Printed and bound by CPI Group (UK) Ltd, Croydon, CR0 4YY

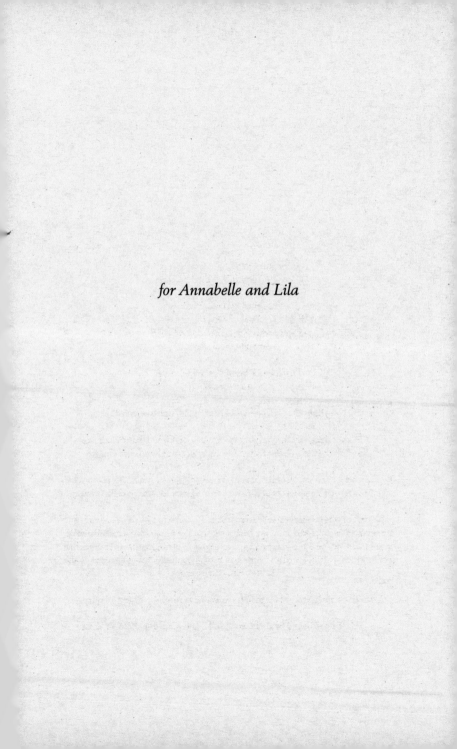

for Annabelle and Lila

Everything flows and nothing abides

HERACLITUS

CONTENTS

SOLSTICE

As Adam steps outside the cold strikes him like a physical thing, the shock still startling after all these weeks. For a moment he pauses, looking out across the bay, the crowding floes of ice. Then, adjusting his goggles, he descends the short ramp to the scoured stone upon which the building stands and strikes out towards the headland.

It is quiet out here today, the only sounds that disturb the silence those of the wind, the occasional squalling cry of the birds. Down by the water an elephant seal lies on the rocks, its vast bulk mottled and sluglike; around it tracks of human activity scar the snow like rust, turning it grey and red and dirty.

In the building behind him the other personnel are celebrating the solstice, an occurrence those stationed here have long observed with an extended meal and drinking and dancing. The event is a way of marking not just the date but the peculiar rhythms of life at the base, the annual cycle which means that from here on the arrivals will slow and departures increase, until only the skeleton crew who maintain the facility through the months of cold and darkness remain.

Passing the Klein-blue boxes of the power distribution units he finds himself wondering again about this tradition. Humans have observed the solstice for tens of thousands of years, but are those festivities truly celebrations, or something more ambivalent? Symbols of loss, of the running down of things? After all, the solstice also marks the beginning of summer's end, the first intimation of the year's long retreat back into the dark.

Beyond the last building the land opens out, the dirty grey of rock and mud and melting snow giving way to the white glare of ice. The wind is stronger here, and even colder, but he does not slow or turn aside; instead, closing his hand around the phone in his pocket, he shrugs his neck deeper into his collar and quickens his step.

Back in Sydney it is just after one, and Ellie will be in the waiting room of the clinic. He can picture her seated in the corner, on the couch she always chooses, trying to concentrate on her tablet or flicking through a magazine. Normally she would not be there alone, but before he left they agreed she would continue the treatment while he was away, a decision he tried not to take as a sign his presence was no longer really needed.

Today's appointment is the last for this cycle and in many ways the only one that matters. For while over the past fortnight Ellie has been to the clinic almost daily, initially for hormone injections, then later for the extraction of the ova and the implantation of the fertilised embryos, it is today that they will take her blood one last time and tell her whether the process has succeeded.

They have been here before, of course. Once a month for the best part of two years the two of them have sat in that office and watched the gynaecologist purse her lips and assume the mask of bland concern she uses to deliver the bad news; once a month for the best part of two years he has reached out to take Ellie's hand as she nods and thanks the gynaecologist, the only sign of her distress the stiffness with which she holds herself, the care with which she finds her way to her feet and back to the waiting room.

It often seems strange to him that they have ended up here. Six years ago, when he and Ellie met, the idea of children seemed impossibly remote, the question of whether he might one day want them so removed from his life as to be irrelevant.

5

Even after all that has happened, the fact of their meeting still seems miraculous to him, a gift. Ellie was at art school, preparing an installation about botanical biodiversity. Looking for images, she contacted the university and was referred to Adam's supervisor, who in turn passed her request to Adam's officemate. Finally, fortuitously, it was passed to Adam himself.

Deep in the final months of his doctorate, he really only scanned the request, then, after making a note about meeting her a few days later, forgot about it so completely that when he arrived at his office to find her seated on the chair under the window he didn't realise she was there for him.

She was dressed in a short skirt, leggings and boots, her dark hair pulled back in a loose ponytail, although it wasn't her outfit that caught his attention at first, but the clarity and directness of her gaze, the ease with which she seemed to inhabit the space around her. Aware she seemed to be expecting him, he stopped and half turned towards her.

'Adam?' she said. 'I'm Ellie.'

He smiled back, aware she could see he didn't know who she was.

'From the College of Fine Art? You told me to come by?'

'Yes,' he said as it came back to him in a rush. 'I'm sorry, I'd forgotten.'

'If now's not a good time . . .' But he waved her down.

'No, now is fine. Just let me get the door open.'

Inside, while he started up his computer, she leaned towards the card pinned to the wall above it, a nineteenth-century drawing of a radiolarian. Rendered in careful pen and ink, its sea-urchin-like form had the delicate perfection of a jewel.

'It's Haeckel, isn't it?' she said, as much to herself as to him.

He glanced up. 'It is. How did you know?'

She smiled. 'I've spent a lot of time looking at the period.'

Leaning over he reached for the card, traced the outline of the image with his finger. 'Is this the sort of thing you're after?'

'Perhaps. I'm interested in the different ways we perceive and represent plants and animals, the way encountering those representations can sometimes be like glimpsing a lost world, all of its own.'

Intrigued, he studied her for a moment. Then he stood up. 'Let me see what I can help you find.'

Over the next two hours he showed her through the

various collections held by the department, increasingly delighted not just by her interest but by the quality of her attention, the care with which she considered each new document or specimen. And so it was unexpected when, as they neared the end of the tour, she turned to him and asked, 'Doesn't it frighten you?'

'Doesn't what frighten me?'

'That these sorts of collections might be all we have left?'

The truth was it terrified him, but he knew no way of giving that fear expression without it overwhelming him. So he just nodded. 'Better we have a record of what's lost.'

In the days that followed they began to correspond by email, her requests for further information and his ideas about other specimens and images that might interest her quickly taking on a playful intimacy, until late one evening, a fortnight after that first meeting, she suggested he meet her at an exhibition the next day.

He was surprised when he first saw her walking towards him. After two weeks chatting online she seemed different: smaller, less perfectly composed. Although she moved with the same confidence, in the light outside the gallery her pale skin was more battered than he remembered, scattered here and there with freckles. Later he learned that she had the same reaction, that like him she had found speaking in person awkward at first, the immediacy of their online friendship replaced by an uneasy combination of familiarity and unfamiliarity.

The exhibition was by a Japanese artist – delicate forms carved from wood and shell and metal poised midway between the biological and the mechanical, that seemed simultaneously ancient and exquisitely modern. Some resembled the skeletons of mammals or birds or fish, others less easily categorised creatures with sleek carapaces of burnished timber, or shimmering skeins of mother-of-pearl, like refugees from the ancient oceans of the Cambrian, or perhaps some strange future in which matter itself had taken on life and inscrutable purpose.

Astonished by their beauty, confused by their alienness, Adam wandered from one to the next, barely speaking. At one point he glanced at Ellie and, catching her watching him, smiled, the fact of her presence suddenly marvellous to him, his delight amplified when she smiled back.

Later, over coffee, he found himself telling her things he had not spoken about to anyone, unravelling the tangle of his feelings about his friend Vann's death the year before, his sense that his doctoral research had gone somehow off course. She in turn revealed details about herself. About losing her mother as a teenager, her attempts to erase herself in the aftermath; about her father and his second, much younger wife, and Ellie's dislike and suspicion of their relationship, her sense that she was the wrong woman for him.

And when the day was done and they were parting, she leaned in and kissed him, her hands against his chest, the gesture so direct, so certain, that for a moment or two he was too startled to respond. Sensing his hesitation she pulled back, waiting for him to recover himself, and then she was kissing him again, deeper this time.

What is most remarkable to him now about those early days is how easy it was, the way they just seemed to mesh. Even the sex, when it happened, was without tension or uncertainty, although not without passion. Within a week they were sleeping together, within a month he was living with her in the old garage she rented in Marrickville, the two of them already like old friends save for the urgency of their physical relationship, the wonder of each other's bodies.

Their first year passed almost without them noticing. He worked on his thesis, huddled over his laptop at a desk under the high windows, while she wrote and modelled her creations on her computer. Unlike many of her contemporaries she was prepared to farm work out, to employ Chinese and Indian and Pakistani programmers to build the things she imagined, leaving her to concentrate on the larger picture and on the music.

Towards the end of their second year together she received her first commission as part of a festival in Singapore; less than a week later Adam was offered a position in a new multidisciplinary research group. And so, though neither was quite sure how it happened, they found themselves a couple with careers and a future.

At the same time it became clear that the social landscape around them was changing as well, as friends married or entered into commitment ceremonies of one kind or another. They discussed doing something similar but neither of them saw the point, and once they'd bought their first apartment it hardly seemed relevant.

But then, in the winter of their third year together, Ellie's friend Holly collapsed outside a café on King Street. Helped to her feet by strangers, she was taken to hospital and diagnosed with a brain tumour. A week later she was dead.

In the days afterwards, Holly's friends rallied together, trying to make sense of her sudden absence. For Ellie in particular it was inconceivable that Holly was gone: they had known each other since childhood, their lives overlapping so much it was almost impossible to imagine herself without Holly.

At least at first Adam expected Ellie to fall apart, but instead she lost herself in work, retreating from him and the world. Worried about her, he tried to draw her back, to find ways of discussing what had happened, but as the weeks turned into months she grew ever more remote.

He was unprepared therefore when one night just before Christmas she told him she wanted a child. They had discussed the question in the past, agreeing that while both of them liked the idea in principle there was no need to rush to a decision. But that night, as he listened to her explaining she didn't want to wait any longer, that she was scared her life was slipping away from her, he realised he had misunderstood – her grief had left her more unanchored than he had known.

He wasn't against the idea, or not in any way he could easily articulate. Yet even as he agreed they would give up contraception, he found himself wondering whether it was the right decision, whether they were moving too quickly or acting for the wrong reasons. Perhaps this was why he didn't pay much attention to her failure to conceive at first. After so many years on the pill it seemed reasonable to assume she would not return to fertility immediately, and that even once she had, the occasional gaps in their lovemaking would mean it was always possible they had simply missed the window for conception. But by the fourth or fifth month Ellie was concerned enough to start counting dates, and insisting they have sex on particular days.

The first time they had this duty sex it was funny. Ellie climbed into bed, settled herself beside him and told him he had to get to work. He laughed, and lifting himself on one elbow to look at her, asked whether this was how it was going to be from now on.

The sex that night was pleasant enough although she seemed distant, preoccupied. When they were done she rolled over and looked at the ceiling.

'Are you okay?' he asked, and in the seconds that lapsed before she answered he understood that she wasn't, not really.

They waited another three months before seeing a doctor. As the two of them walked into the clinic, they didn't touch, their bodies discrete in a way that was new to him. The consultation was professional, even polished, the doctor's manner making it clear that while she had had this conversation many times before, they had her full attention now. As the doctor spoke she made eye contact with both of them, pausing every few sentences to emphasise some particular point. In the chair beside him Ellie sat in silence, her body tense and still, with a focus he had not noticed before.

Looking back now he wonders if that was the moment he began to feel she had changed in some fundamental way, as if the woman he knew had been replaced by somebody he no longer understood.

At their second consultation the doctor told them there was no clear reason for their failure to conceive, and suggested they move straight into the program. Ellie's eyes met his. Startled, he hesitated, the costs of the procedure confusing him.

'Yes,' he said, 'of course.'

Driving home he listened as she ran through the options and scenarios the doctor had outlined, repeating them to him as if to fix them in her memory. She had found the doctor's words encouraging, even exciting, and he knew she wanted him to share in that excitement. But instead he found himself pulling back, offering only vague words of caution, until at last she paused.

'If you're not okay with this you should say.'

He smiled. 'Of course I'm okay with it.'

'Are you sure?' she asked. He could feel her staring at him.

'I'm sure.'

And he was, at least when he spoke, although he found himself growing less certain the first time Ellie underwent the harvesting. Strapped into the chair, she looked so small, so vulnerable, he wanted to push the doctors aside, leave the clinic and never return. Yet when he caught her eye he saw a ferocity that frightened him.

It didn't work. Not that time, nor the next, nor the many that came after. And with each failed attempt he felt the distance between them grow. Ellie grew thinner, more tired, more aloof. Although they went through the motions, it often seemed their life together had been reduced to this enervating cycle of biology and technology, the ease they shared replaced by a wanting that was almost like pain. When they fucked she would close her eyes, moving above him in silence, her entire body focused not on the act but on something inward, something she needed but could not reach, until the release she was seeking shuddered through her. Sometimes that intensity frightened him, but afterwards, when she turned away, eager to lose herself in the oblivion of sleep, he felt her withdrawal as a kind of loss, so complete it was almost physical.

Others saw little of this. When they first entered the program she was determined to be open about the treatments. 'I don't want to be lying about why I'm sick or tired, or hiding things from my friends,' she said when he questioned the wisdom of being so public about the process. But as the months passed and the unsuccessful attempts multiplied, they began to be more circumspect, avoiding the subject socially whenever possible, becoming vague about the details. Sharing the truth was too difficult, too exposing.

He came to recognise the signs, the solicitous pause or awkward shift in emotional register that preceded people's questions. Their masks of concern when he told them he'd rather not talk about it, the careful conversation as he walked away. Sometimes he could see the question in their eyes: Was it he who had the problem? Or was it her? And in those moments he felt himself growing angry, chafing against their pity, their assumption that there was something wrong with either of them, until having to fight not to grow terse or lose his temper became a regular occurrence.

Yet worse were the well-meaning pieces of advice, the recommendations they speak to a particular naturopath, or investigate natural remedies of one sort or another. 'She told me I should eat bananas before sex,' Ellie would say as they walked home after a dinner. Or: 'Anna said her trainer recommends yoga to strengthen the womb,' and while their laughter often briefly united them, the truth was that these sorts of ideas had become a point of tension, Ellie's need to invest events with meaning conflicting with his scientific approach to the variables.

This sense of shared isolation bound them together to some extent, but within it they had never been further apart. Absorbed by new commissions and teaching, Ellie retreated ever further into her work, and Adam spent longer and longer hours at the university, or travelling to conferences and meetings.

Meanwhile Adam found himself searching for new reasons to resist. Unlike some of his colleagues he had never succumbed to despair over the changing climate, preferring to believe that, faced with looming disaster, politicians and business leaders would be forced to look for solutions. But as the situation grew ever more urgent he found himself increasingly alarmed about what was to come. Each week there seemed to be new evidence that the process was hastening. In the Arctic the permafrost was melting; in Greenland and Antarctica the ice sheets were destabilising, their deterioration outpacing even the most pessimistic models; in the Atlantic the currents were growing more erratic, slowing down and shifting. Even the oceans themselves seemed to be dying, their waters more acidic by the month.

One day in his office he reviewed a new study about the release of methane from the ocean floor and saw, more starkly than ever before, the conundrum the world faced. It wasn't simply that they needed to consume less, to bring humanity's impact on the biosphere under control, it was that there were just too many people, and even allowing for technological change and economic restructuring, the planet was on a collision course with disaster. In the United States and India floods covered millions of square kilometres, in Africa and Europe the heat was growing ever more intense, in Indonesia and Brazil and Malaysia the forests were burning, yet he and Ellie were trying to have a baby. What sort of world would that child inherit? Were they really doing the right thing by bringing another life into it?

That night at home they argued, not about these questions, nor even the treatment, but over money and family, Adam needling Ellie over her refusal to try to get along with her father's new wife, knowing as he did that he was provoking her, that she felt betrayed by him not taking her side. But even as they rehearsed their irritation with each other he could not get the equations he had scribbled down out of his head, could not let go of the fact that bringing one more mouth into the world was merely adding to a problem that was already out of control. One of his colleagues sometimes talked about the deep structures of intelligence, the way in which human brains had been shaped by evolution. 'We don't change because we don't believe in the problem,' he would say, 'at least not at the deep, intuitive level we need to. We can see it when it's in front of us, see what it means; we know we have to change. But as soon as we're away from it our old thinking reasserts itself, our desire to reproduce, to build power.'

In the past some semblance of ease had always reasserted itself following an argument, but after that night they seemed unable to find a new equilibrium. And so when Adam was offered the chance to be part of an expedition to the Antarctic he took it immediately, looking forward to the opportunity to lose himself in something new.

The project he is attached to is attempting to develop a better understanding of the continent's climate during previous periods of warming, using fossilised plants and traces of ancient pollen to chart the transformation of the landscape, its transition from rainforest to tundra and finally the barrenness that now surrounds him. And while for the most part the work of gathering samples of sediment and rock has been routine, the experience has been anything but. Travelling south he watched the temperate seas give way to the heaving swells of the Southern Ocean, the water growing darker, denser, heavier, before it changed again, the massive swells replaced first by icebergs and then by fields of drifting ice, their surfaces sculpted by wind and waves, until at last the dark bluffs and gleaming snow of the continent itself hove into view.

The nature of their work means the occasions when he and his fellow scientists are able to articulate the effect of the place upon them are few, but he knows he is not the only one who feels themselves altered by it, or that their work here is bringing them close to something pure, something normally obscured. On a noticeboard someone has pinned a piece of paper bearing the words 'the emptier the land, the more luminous and precise the names for its features', and although he is not sure where the line comes from he recognises it in some deep way, for it captures his feeling he is in a place of the infinite, a place that exists without reference to the human, or indeed to any notion beyond the great wheel of the seasons, the ceaseless motion of the ice. Walking alone along the headland by the base, where orcas can sometimes be seen playing offshore, their piebald bodies bobbing up and down like the horses on a fairground ride, or around the edge of the bay where the only sound is that of the skuas and the wind, it is possible to feel his anger and unhappiness wash away.

The others feel the same, he is certain of it. It is visible in the way they suddenly grin and laugh, as if alive in a way they haven't been before. But he also knows they share the urgency of what they do, that beneath their banter lies an awareness that they are at the end of something. This year the ice has retreated further than ever, exposing rock and stone buried for millions of years. To the east and west the glaciers are flowing faster and faster, calving bergs half the size of cities day after day, a process of transformation so vast it is difficult to comprehend.

Indeed, sometimes it seems the entire continent is moving around them. Just over a week ago he flew out with a team assigned to take samples from the shelf to the west of the station. It was a long flight, three hours tracking out across the whiteness, yet for the most part it passed in silence, Adam and the others absorbed in the landscape passing beneath them.

When they landed at their destination Adam was the first one out, clambering down quickly, his head bent low to avoid the rotors, the thunderous whine of the turbines. But as the roar of the engine faded it was replaced by another sound, a deep, geological creaking and groaning that rose and fell and echoed to the horizon.

Turning back to the helicopter, Adam saw that the others heard it too, that he was not imagining it. And he understood what it was, that the sound was the ice shifting beneath them as the entire landscape on which they stood slipped and fell towards the sea.

That night he hardly slept, the implications of what he had heard chasing through his mind. He knew he should have been terrified, or in despair, yet instead he felt a kind of elation, as if he had been freed somehow.

The next morning he rose early, hoping to catch Ellie before work, excited by his returned desire for her, his sense that they were not wrong to be doing this thing. But when he phoned she was already at the clinic for her hormone shots, unable to talk. 'I'll call you,' she said, 'when I get the result.'

And so, a week later, he is here, waiting. To the north the sun is growing slowly, imperceptibly lower, the apogee of its long transit across the sky finally past, its long progress downward begun. But although winter is approaching, it will not be forever, and in its wake summer will come again, and again, each warmer than the last, each bringing with it the promise of change, of loss. They will have the child, or not, he thinks, and the world will go on, and they will go on, and he will love her and they will see where tomorrow takes them. For what else is there to do, except hang on, and hope?

Overhead the sun shines, white and weakly warm against his face; to the south the ice is moving, to the north the sea spreads out into the future.

And in his hand the phone begins to ring.

MONSOON

He wakes to heat, the seeping light of the sun against the blinds. On his nightstand the clock reads 5:42. He feels confused, unanchored in time.

Sitting up he looks around. Although the other half of the bed is empty, he does not remember Ellie getting up, does not remember anything beyond the usual nocturnal confusion of broken sleep and unsettled dreams.

Out in the hall he makes his way towards the kitchen, listening for the sound of Ellie's voice as he steps around the clothes and toys left scattered and abandoned the day before. When he opens the door Summer is seated at the table, cup of juice in one hand. Seeing him she grins, shouts, 'Daddy!'

Leaning down he kisses her on the head, then turns to Ellie. 'How long have you been up?'

She looks drawn, the skin beneath her eyes bruised. 'A while.'

He pulls the fridge open and the seal gives a flat, deflated sound. 'Power off again?'

'Since midnight.'

Pouring himself a glass of juice he sits down, lifts Summer onto his lap and takes an experimental sip. 'The food will be spoiled.'

Ellie shoots him a barbed look. 'Really? That hadn't occurred to me.'

He puts down his glass. They have had to empty and restock the fridge half a dozen times in the past month alone.

'Sorry,' Ellie sighs, lifting a hand.

'Don't worry about it. Any word on when it will be back on?'

She shakes her head. 'Not yet.'

'I'll check the updates,' Adam says, taking out his phone.

'Didn't I just say there wasn't anything?' she says, the edge in her tone enough to make both of them fall still.

For a few seconds they sit staring at each other. Then Ellie turns away.

'Do you want to go back to bed?' he asks.

'I won't sleep.'

'Are you sure?'

'Maybe when the power comes back on.'

On his knee Summer is wriggling about, grabbing at his face. Giving her his hand he lets her grab his finger instead, opening his mouth in a playful mockery of pain.

It is the third power cut this week, the tenth or eleventh since the beginning of the month. For the past few summers there have been intermittent outages caused by the ever-increasing demand for air-conditioning, but the fires of recent months have damaged the lines, making brownouts and outright power failures common.

On the other side of the table Ellie begins clearing the remains of breakfast. Adam looks up.

'I'll do that.'

'It's fine. I've got it.'

'Really,' he says, setting Summer down and standing. 'I'm happy to.'

'I said I'm fine.'

Summer looks startled by Ellie's tone. Adam doesn't move. Finally he backs away. 'I should have a shower,' he says. 'I've got work to do.'

In the half-light of the bathroom he lets the cool water wash over him, playing the exchange with Ellie back over, and again. Sometimes it frightens him, the way conversations loop and repeat in his mind, increasing his sense of grievance with every repetition, and today is no exception. It is no secret to either of them that Ellie is struggling, but despite talking about it numerous times, she refuses to get help.

As he dries himself he tries to put the scene in the kitchen out of his mind and concentrate on work. Since his return from Antarctica Adam's research group have been attached to an international project that is attempting to model the changes to the South Asian monsoon. For the best part of two decades scientists have been worried about its growing unpredictability, and last year their worst fears were realised. The rains that usually arrived in July or August failed to appear, leaving the subcontinent to bake in record heat. Crops failed, leading to food shortages and starvation. Then in November torrential rain and massive floods killed more than a million and left another hundred million homeless. And finally, in the aftermath, the economy collapsed, leading to the widespread unemployment that is behind the riots in Mumbai and Calcutta in recent weeks.

Adam still finds the scale of the disaster difficult to comprehend. Yet with each passing week it seems more likely this year will be worse: although it is only March, temperatures in the Indian Ocean have already surpassed the records set last year, and the heat is building rapidly on the land. For the members of the team in New Delhi this lends the project a powerful, even frightening urgency, an urgency Adam finds it increasingly difficult not to share.

Once he is dressed he opens his computer, scans the emails that crowd his inbox. Because his colleagues are separated by half a dozen time zones, every morning brings new material to work on, and before long Adam is so absorbed in reading the latest reports he doesn't hear Ellie until she appears at the door, her face ashen.

'What is it?' he asks, getting to his feet.

'It's Summer, she's having an asthma attack.'

'Her puffer isn't helping?'

'Not enough. I think we need to get her to hospital.'

Following Ellie down the hall, Adam finds Summer lying on the couch, her back arched, eyes half closed. Slipping an arm under her he scoops her up.

'You grab her things,' he says to Ellie. 'I'll get her out to the car.'

Although it is still early the traffic is heavy, cars banked up in long lines where the lights have failed. Forcing himself to stay calm, he tries to concentrate on the road ahead, but every time he glances in the mirror Ellie is staring at him.

At the hospital he pulls up outside Emergency. 'You get her inside,' he says. 'I'll go park the car.'

A few minutes later he is back. The waiting room is crowded, people slumped in the plastic seats that line the space, fanning themselves with bits of paper and staring at their phones or the televisions overhead. Ellie is by the triage desk, Summer in her arms. He hurries towards her, arriving in time to see the nurse behind the perspex window lean forward and gesture to the security door on the right, which stands propped open with a chair in the absence of power.

The corridor beyond the door is dim, the emergency lights giving the space an almost submarine hue. As they enter, a nurse appears from one of the rooms on the left.

'Asthma?' he asks.

'Yes,' Ellie says, falling into the formal yet slightly deferential tone she tends to assume around figures of authority.

'Has she had episodes like this before?'

Adam and Ellie exchange glances. 'Never this bad,' Adam says, speaking for them both.

The nurse motions to a pair of plastic chairs by the wall. 'Take a seat over there and I'll get the doctor,' he says.

They sit down as directed. Summer's breath comes in shallow gasps and the skin around her mouth is blue. Pressing her lips to Summer's hair, Ellie strokes her arm with her free hand.

'It's okay, sweetie,' she says, 'the doctor will be here soon.' As she speaks she leans forward, rocking gently in her seat, her face intent.

Adam considers reaching out, drawing her to him, but he knows this look well enough to know she does not want him to, that even if she acceded to his touch it would be stiffly, unnaturally.

A moment later the nurse reappears, the doctor behind him. Handing the screen she holds to the nurse, the doctor kneels down in front of them.

'This is Summer?' she asks.

'Yes,' Ellie says.

'How long has she been like this?'

'An hour or so.'

'Hi, Summer,' the doctor says. 'I'm just going to have a look at your chest, okay?'

When she doesn't get a reply she pulls the child's T-shirt up. Summer's chest and abdomen are bulging and expanding, the skin straining against her ribs with the effort of breathing.

'She's had Ventolin already?'

'Yes,' Ellie says, 'but it doesn't seem to have helped.'

The doctor gives a quick nod, then stands up. 'Okay,' she says in a quick, clipped voice. 'We need to get her connected to a monitor. Then we'll give her medication to open up her airways.'

They carry her to a bed in one of the alcoves and stand back while the nurse attaches a monitor to Summer's finger and presses a pair of cannulas into her nose, murmuring comfortingly when she flinches. Then, with one eye on the monitor, he and the doctor prepare an inhaler and administer a spray, waiting for a few seconds before coaxing her to swallow a thick syrup, a process that makes Summer cough and gag several times before she succeeds, the sticky pink liquid spilling out and coating her chin and neck. In the silence after the coughing stops the doctor explains that the nurse will be back in a few minutes to check on them.

'Will she be okay?' Ellie asks, getting to her feet.

'I hope so,' the doctor says. 'But we won't know for a while.'

Left alone the two of them barely speak, just watch and wait. Seated on the bed beside Summer, Ellie strokes her daughter's hair, her whole attention focused on the act, as if it might be possible to fix her by sheer force of will.

Although it continues to come in shallow gasps, over the next half an hour or so Summer's breathing grows easier, until almost without warning she opens her eyes.

For a moment Adam thinks he will weep, his relief is so

intense. Leaning forward he touches Summer's arm, while Ellie kisses her forehead.

'Hey sweetie,' she says, her voice cracking.

There is talk of keeping her overnight, but the hospital is crowded, its capacity stretched to the limit, so just after seven they are released with new puffers and instructions to return if there are further difficulties.

By the time they get home it is almost eight. When they open the door the house is hot, the air thick with the stink of rotting food. Adam flicks a switch and the hall fills with light.

'Power's back at least,' he says. 'Let me get the garbage outside; we can deal with the fridge once Summer's in bed.'

While he loads the bin he listens to Ellie getting Summer into her nightie. Usually she resists bedtime, seeking to delay the day's end as long as possible, but tonight she is asleep almost as soon as she lies down.

Back in the living room he flicks the television on. As it has been for weeks, the news is about the power cuts and the climate negotiations in Bangkok, which have reached an impasse yet again. The report from Thailand is followed by items about unexplained fish deaths in Tasmania and Victoria, and yet another story about the sudden bird die-offs in the west. But a moment later the images of dead birds are replaced by an interview with a newspaper columnist who has just published a book arguing that the evidence for the planet's warming is flawed, that in fact it is entering a phase of rapid cooling. Adam watches with fury boiling up in him at the man's bland reasonableness, his polished deceit.

'Why are they showing this crap?' he demands, his voice raised.

Behind him in the kitchen Ellie makes an exasperated noise. 'Just turn it off,' she says.

'I mean, why give these idiots a platform?'

When Ellie doesn't reply he snaps at the television to mute it, and turns to face her. 'They blather on about representing all sides of an issue but they reduce everything to talking heads and arguments about the science.'

'The media are shit, everybody knows that.'

'They're not just shit, they're irresponsible. No, more than that, they're dangerous. It's not just that they're scientifically ignorant, it's that they work to actively obstruct change. They're like a cancer.'

'I agree.'

He stares at her. 'That's all you've got to say?'

She stares at him, unmoving. 'Please, Adam.'

'What?'

'I'm not going to argue with you.'

'I don't want to argue. I'm just frustrated.'

But even as he speaks he knows he's lying, that he does want to fight. Because he's angry, and it isn't just the television or his work or the fact that the world is coming unravelled, it's Ellie. It isn't fair, but her passivity, her refusal to engage with him, to react, infuriates him.

'You think it's okay then? That they give this moron airtime?' he demands.

'No. But I think you get off on being angry. Sometimes it's like you actually want the worst to happen because it will mean you're right, and the world *is* fucked.'

'That's not fair,' says Adam. But he knows Ellie is right, that part of him enjoys the disaster, the constant confirmation of his worst fears.

'Fuck fair,' Ellie says. 'I'm sick of it. Sick of your anger. Sick of you blaming me for everything.'

Adam stands unspeaking. He knows he wants this, wants the confrontation, but he holds back, afraid of the consequences.

'Forget it,' he says at last. 'I'm going out.'

Ellie stares at him. 'Whatever,' she says.

Outside it is dark but no cooler, the promised change still several hours off. Standing in the driveway he is uncertain whether to drive or walk, until the weight of the keys in his pocket decides him.

As he reverses out he cannot help but see Summer's seat in the back, the jumble of toys and crumbled biscuits surrounding it. They had bought the car a few weeks before she was born, and as they drove home after having it fitted with the booster seat, Adam found himself fighting the impulse to keep looking over his shoulder at it, this visual evidence that he had been transformed into a suburban father.

That feeling returns as he pulls away down the street, intensified by the mess of the day. Before he left home in his second year of university his parents used to lend him their car, and across the long summers he would spend his evenings cruising the streets, careless in the freedom of movement. For a time he'd had a passion for the music of the late 1960s and early seventies, the back catalogue of the Stones and Bowie and the Velvet Underground, and driving alone he played them over and over, watching the city spool by through his open window, feeling the breeze, the smell of the hot asphalt, as 'Gimme Shelter' and 'Queen Bitch' and 'Sweet Jane' filled the car.

Sometimes he wonders whether there is something viral about music, the way it erases the space of time between the present and the past selves that inhabit us, because even now he has only to hear those tracks and it all comes back, all that longing and desire, all that hunger for something pure and transcendent and beautiful. Wanting that now he dials up *Aladdin Sane*, allowing the first pulse of 'Watch That Man' to release him as he angles through the traffic, pushing on past the other cars in the warm dark, watching the play of their lights, the drivers caught up in their private worlds as they sit huddled over their wheels. Most nights when he does this it is liberating, but tonight he cannot shake the feeling that he is losing something he doesn't want to lose but no longer knows how to hang onto. It isn't just about Ellie, of course, although that's a lot of it, it's the sense that things are breaking down, spiralling out of control, and his own powerlessness to do anything about it. More and more he feels like he does not know the person he is becoming, that he is falling faster and faster without any idea of where and when he will land.

Nor is it just him. All summer Ellie has been working on a project about Alzheimer's and the erasure of the past. At first it was a series of sculptures created out of the faces of sufferers, their features smoothed away here and there, but it has developed to incorporate other components: brain scans showing the plaque on the dendrites; books filled with pages from which most of the text has been obliterated, leaving only random phrases and words; video loops of people shouting and weeping, or lost in the arrested rigidity of advanced Alzheimer's, their faces collapsed in on themselves, the only expression the flickering of the eyelids, the occasional protrusion of a tongue or the restless formation of some incomprehensible muttering.

Exactly why she is doing this now is not clear to him, but it frightens him to see her so absorbed in a project which is about the loss of the self, the annihilation of memory, suggesting as it does some desire to escape the present.

Yet he also knows it is not she who is to blame. He is the one who seems unable to adapt to family life, to find an equilibrium that will let him be the parent he knows he should be. It is not that he doesn't want to, just that no matter how hard he tries, it seems to elude him. And so he removes himself emotionally, physically, only returning in order to provoke scenes like tonight's.

It is almost midnight by the time he eases the car back into the drive. Inside, the house is dark, the only sound the low whirr of the fridge. Halfway along the hall he pauses at Summer's door. She lies sprawled sideways across the bed, face down; for a moment he stands unmoving, marvelling at the wonder of her, of the way sleep seems to take her so completely.

Outside his and Ellie's bedroom he hesitates, uncertain whether he should turn around and sleep on the couch, but then he steps in, undressing quietly and sliding in beside her.

Although she does not move he can tell by the rhythm of her breathing that she is awake, the cool flesh of her body alert. In the darkness he can see the outline of her hip beneath the sheet, the pale skin of her shoulders. He could reach out, let his hand touch her; that would be enough to make her turn to him, let them begin to dissolve their anger in the familiar intimacy of each other's body. But he knows already he will not; instead he will lie here staring at the ceiling, waiting for her to slip away into sleep next to him.

Somewhere in the distance thunder rumbles. Overhead the first drops of rain.

CLADE

It is almost five when Maddie hears the car on the drive, and the afternoon wind is already up, the trees shifting and breathing in long restless waves. For a few seconds she doesn't move, just sits listening, unwilling to relinquish her privacy quite yet. Then, steeling herself, she sets down her screen and stands.

Summer is out of the car by the time Maddie reaches the door, looking around with the awkwardness of the thirteen-year-old she has recently become. Her ears are covered by bulky headphones, half concealed by a striped woollen hat, its presence incongruous given her bare legs and thongs. Seeing Maddie, her face creases into an uncertain half-smile.

Although its source has never been clear to Maddie there has been a core of sadness and restlessness in Summer for as long as she can recall, and looking at her now she sees it has not dissipated, has if anything grown more pronounced.

On the driver's side Ellie has emerged as well. Maddie has not seen her stepdaughter since Tom's funeral and she knows she should go to her, embrace her, but before she can the moment passes.

'Sorry we're late,' Ellie says, her voice tense. 'It took forever to get away.'

'I was worried you'd changed your mind.'

'Of course not.'

'You're still planning to stay then?' Maddie says, catching herself too late. 'I mean, I hope you're still planning to stay.'

Ellie regards her warily. 'Only if it's okay?'

'Absolutely,' Maddie says, stepping forward. 'Here, let me help you with the bags.'

Because Summer is eager to swim they unpack quickly and head down to the beach, following the road to the bend and then cutting sideways through the blackbutt trees to the wooden pathway that extends over the old creek bed. Out over the water the sky is already a deep, gorgeous red, legacy of the eruptions in the Philippines and Indonesia and the fires in Borneo and Sumatra, and Maddie remembers a holiday with Tom in Kashmir, the colour of the lakes at dawn.

Until the summer before last the pathway was the easiest way onto the sand, but as the storms have grown more frequent the rising water has carried off more and more of the beach, meaning the pathway now hangs suspended a metre or two above the ground, its frame twisted and buckled like a broken rollercoaster. There have been meetings about the situation, petitions demanding the sand be replaced and anti-erosion measures strengthened, but Maddie has not joined the protests. At first that was because she could not find it in herself to care, but more recently it is because she has come to feel there is something beautiful in this ruination of the beach, a sense in which its destruction answers a need within her.

As they reach the sand Summer bounces ahead, pulling off her singlet. The whole way down she has been distant, dawdling several metres behind the older women, avoiding their attempts to engage her in conversation, but now she is like a child again.

'Leave your stuff over there,' Ellie says, pointing to a spot down by the rocks.

But Summer is already off, sprinting across the sand towards the water. As a child she was amazingly physical, her thin body tense with a restless energy that only seemed bearable when she was able to lose herself in motion.

Seeing her sudden joy as she runs, the careless fluidity of her stride, Maddie realises little has changed.

'She looks happy,' she says.

Ellie stares after Summer's receding form. 'She's been in a foul mood all day.'

'About what?'

At the water's edge Summer bounds out into the waves, her long steps shortening as the water grows deeper, until at last she drops into a low, clean dive and disappears.

'Just the usual teenage shit,' Ellie says, putting her bag beside Summer's towel. 'I'm sorry she was so rude on the way down. She's been looking forward to seeing you for weeks.'

'Don't worry about it. I'm always pleased to see her.'

'The past couple of months haven't been easy for her. She was close to Dad.'

When Maddie doesn't reply she glances after Summer. 'I sometimes wonder what it means to someone her age. She keeps so much inside I worry about how it's affecting her.'

'She spoke beautifully at his funeral.'

Ellie smiles. 'She did. He would have been proud of her.'

'He was proud of you as well. You know that, don't you?'

Behind her sunglasses Ellie's face tightens and Maddie knows she has overstepped, assumed too much.

But Ellie just says, 'Do you want to swim?'

'Sure,' Maddie replies.

It is growing dark by the time they get back to the house, and while Summer disappears to her room and Ellie takes a shower, Maddie prepares dinner. Although she eats at home most nights it is strange to be cooking for others again, the rhythms somehow off. As she is chopping tomatoes Ellie appears, a towel wrapped around her head.

'Do you need a hand?' she asks, but Maddie shakes her head.

'I'm fine.'

'Really,' Ellie says. 'I'd like to help.'

'No need. It's almost done.'

'Are you sure? I could do the salad.'

Ellie picks up an avocado and before she can stop herself Maddie snatches it back.

'I said I was all right,' she snaps.

Ellie doesn't move, just stands staring at her. Maddie flushes.

'I'm sorry,' she begins, but Ellie is already backing away.

'Don't worry about it,' she says.

It is more than fifteen years since Tom came back from a weekend surfing trip to tell her he had put the deposit down on a beach house. At the time they had been married for almost five years, and although she had grown used to his impulsiveness this was a new order of recklessness, even for him. But when she accompanied him the next weekend she found herself won over, both by the place itself and by Tom's unfeigned enthusiasm for it.

At first the idea was that it would be a retreat for the two of them, but as the months passed and they began to spend more time here, Tom took to inviting friends to join them. For Maddie these visits were often stressful, but Tom revelled in the unstructured days and long afternoons and evenings of rambling conversation they gave rise to.

Yet while they regularly had friends down, Ellie never came. It wasn't for want of trying: every few months Tom would suggest she and Adam join them for a few days, but Ellie always found excuses, evading her father's invitations in the same way she did all his overtures.

Although she tried, Maddie found it difficult to hide her irritation with her stepdaughter. She had not been naïve enough to think Ellie would like the idea of her father marrying a woman only five years older than herself, but from the outset Ellie had been unwelcoming, even hostile. At the time she told herself she was annoyed on Tom's behalf, angry at Ellie for pushing him away, hurting him. But looking back she wonders whether it wasn't more complicated than that, whether in fact she preferred not having Ellie around. Although she knew Tom loved her she was also uneasy about the way his and Ellie's shared memories of Ellie's mother bound the two of them together, connecting them to a past Maddie could never be a part of.

Summer's birth changed all that. From the moment he saw her Tom was smitten with his granddaughter, and so, despite both Ellie and Maddie's separate resistance, she found herself and Tom spending more time with Adam and Ellie.

Usually these meetings took place in neutral settings – in parks or cafés – but sometimes there were visits to Ellie and Adam's house, or, less often, lunch at Maddie and Tom's place in Bondi. It was at one such lunch when Summer was eighteen months old that Tom suggested they all spend a weekend down the coast. While it wasn't the first time the offer had been made, it was the first time it had been made to Ellie and Adam together. Maddie felt herself stiffen, uncertain whether she was angry with Tom for not consulting her first or for making the invitation at all, but Adam grinned and glanced at Ellie and said that sounded great, they'd love to come, as if he couldn't see the way Ellie had fallen still beside him.

When the agreed-upon weekend arrived she headed down a day early and spent the afternoon cleaning and arranging the house and buying food and flowers. Organising the adult bedrooms was easy, but when she came to the room Summer was to stay in she found herself hesitating, brought up short by the realisation she had no clear idea of what was needed. After half an hour's prevarication she drove back into Nowra and bought a cotton bedspread decorated with cartoon bees and old-fashioned hives.

The next day Ellie and Adam arrived late, barely able to look at each other after driving the whole way with Summer screaming in the car. Conscious of how much Tom wanted the weekend to be a success, Maddie insisted it didn't matter, and tried not to look too relieved when Ellie said she had a headache and went to bed early.

She wasn't surprised: she'd been expecting the weekend to be difficult. What she hadn't expected was how much she'd enjoy being with Summer. Although she had friends with children, she'd never really had a lot to do with them, and so tended to be stiff and formal, frightening them off. But when Summer woke up the next morning she was so delighted with the house and the bush at the back it was impossible not to share her pleasure. For much of the first day she rambled about on the lawn picking up sticks and leaves, pausing only to sleep or eat.

After lunch, while Summer slept, Tom asked who wanted to go for a walk. Knowing he wanted time alone with Ellie, Maddie declined, electing to stay behind with Adam. Left alone the two of them chatted, Adam's relaxed mood a relief after the strained atmosphere with Ellie, until eventually Summer emerged, bleary with sleep. At first she clung close to Adam, but as her good humour returned she approached Maddie, leading her to the backyard to join her in some sort of game involving pebbles and shells and sticks, so that when Ellie and Tom returned and Summer ran back to her mother, Adam grinned at Maddie.

'You're good with her,' he said.

Maddie laughed. 'Really?' she asked.

'Really,' Adam said.

That night she lay beside Tom, aware of him awake beside her. Because of their age difference the two of them had only rarely discussed children, and when they had it was usually couched in terms of her ambivalence about the idea. But charged as he was with the success of the day, with the sense of connection and family, she knew it was on his mind.

'That went well,' he said at last, his voice quiet in the dark.

Outside a nightjar called, the sound echoing through the trees.

'Summer is so like Ellie at the same age,' he said when she didn't respond.

She felt a hollow in her belly at his words, an ache almost, and rolling closer she laid her head on his chest. She could hear him holding the words back, knew the struggle it was for him: by nature Tom wanted things to be in the open, to talk about his feelings and to know her mind. It was a desire she often found herself obstructing with little acts of withholding, refusals that shamed her in retrospect not just for their pointlessness, but for their compulsiveness.

'She's lovely,' she said, but Tom didn't reply, just reached up and stroked her hair.

She wakes with the dawn, light flooding into her room. When she and Tom bought the house it was impossible to sleep past sunrise, especially in summer, daybreak bringing kookaburras and cuckoos and swooping flocks of cockatoos, their crazed laughter and screeching clamour echoing through the trees like a memory of the primordial forest. The diversity and profligacy of the birdlife was a big part of what Tom loved about being here, his pleasure in it a source of amusement for the two of them. It was the *thereness* of them he said he loved, their presence and life and total absorption in the moment.

Most of the birds are gone now. She is not sure when they began to disappear: elsewhere there have been huge die-offs, great waves of birds falling from the skies, yet here the process has been more gradual, species slowly disappearing, those that remain less numerous with each passing year.

Although she expected to be the first one up, Ellie is already in the kitchen, a pot of coffee and her screen on the table in front of her. Ellie looks up as she enters and for a second the two of them hesitate, uncomfortable after their edginess last night. Then Ellie gestures towards the coffee.

'I hope you don't mind: it's so long since I had any.'

Maddie nods. Since the crop failures three years ago, coffee has become increasingly expensive and difficult to get.

'Of course not.'

'Would you like some?' Ellie asks.

'That would be nice,' she says.

Taking down a mug she pours herself half a cup, and sits opposite Ellie.

'You're up early.'

Ellie shrugs. 'Most mornings I go to the studio for

an hour or two before Summer wakes up. I find it helpful having that space, before the day begins.'

'What are you reading?'

'Li Po.' Ellie flips her screen over and slides it across the table to Maddie. 'He's a poet, eighth-century Chinese. I've been reading a lot of him.'

Not for the first time Maddie is reminded of the gulf between the two of them, of her sense that her stepdaughter has always thought her life as an artist makes her somehow superior. But she can also see that Ellie is trying, so she musters a smile.

'Was there something you wanted to do today?' she asks.

'Summer will want to go to the beach.'

'Of course. And you?'

'I'm happy to just tag along.'

When Ellie leaves to have a shower Maddie picks up the screen. The poem is called 'The River Merchant's Wife'. Ellie has annotated it here and there, highlighting one passage in particular:

> *I desired my dust to be mingled with yours*
> *Forever and forever and forever.*
> *Why should I climb the lookout?*

Maddie feels a twist of grief. And then, irrationally, a flash of anger at the possibility Ellie may have been thinking of her.

When she learned she was pregnant she let a fortnight pass before she told Tom. Later she pretended she hadn't known immediately, and that once she had she was worried that telling people would make it real, and therefore make her vulnerable, but that wasn't all of it. She also kept it secret because some part of her felt the pregnancy was hers alone, and that every person who knew took a piece of it from her.

She could have gone longer, of course: although it was strange to feel her body changing, the heat in her blood, Tom did not suspect anything until she told him.

As the weeks passed and her body began to thicken she worked hard to conceal it from everyone but him. Tom thought it was concern about growing fat, about losing control, but it had more to do with a lack of desire to discuss her condition with others, to face questions and field looks. She had seen the way pregnancy turned women's bodies into public things, the way strangers assumed the right to touch their bellies or speak to them as familiars, and she recoiled from it, so much so that even in the later months, when the fact was inescapable, she avoided social events, affecting a brightness that was not hers, but armour.

It was a strange time. Later Tom took to saying they grew closer during her pregnancy, but she knew it wasn't that simple. She let Tom see what he needed to see, but still she kept much of what she felt to herself, unwilling to share her savage joy at the thought of the life growing within her.

She did not have a birth plan. Although it amused Tom that somebody as controlling as she was should be so accepting about this one thing, the idea of trying to predict the unpredictable seemed ridiculous to her. And so even as she listened to her friends describing the arrangements they had made, the lists of helpers and midwives and prohibited drugs, or extolling the virtues of natural birth, home birth, midwifery, she found herself wondering whether it might be possible to have the child alone, with nobody but some anonymous doctor in attendance.

In the end it didn't matter because Declan arrived four weeks early, the first contraction occurring at three on a Monday morning. She tried to tell herself it was a firm kick or a roll that had woken her, taking herself to the bathroom in the dark to drink a glass of water. But when the second struck as she was shuffling back to bed she grunted, and Tom started awake.

'It's coming,' she said, and he was already there close to her. This was the last time they would be here like this, she thought as she looked at him looking at her.

'I'll call the hospital,' he said, but she shook her head.

'No,' she said, suddenly afraid of what would come next, 'not yet. Let's wait for a little longer.'

It is nearly eight by the time Summer appears, but by half past they are on the beach. After last night's wind the air is calm, the water blue and glassy, waves slowly crumbling in steady breaths onto the sand. Maddie does not swim often but today she allows herself to be convinced for Summer's sake. Once, she had had no qualms about being seen in a bikini; although she had never obsessed over her body in the way many of her friends did, that was partly because she never really needed to, having been slim and fit since she was a child. Yet as she undresses next to Summer she is aware of how she has aged, the subtle loosening of the flesh, the thickening of her waist.

After a few minutes in the shallows Summer strikes out away from the shore, moving with confident, relaxed strokes. Ellie follows her, keeping pace easily, her body toned by the kilometres she swims each week. Watching them, Maddie is aware that she no longer knows how to find her way into that ease with her body, the steady motion of swimming or running or breathing. Or love.

Just before noon they head into town. Until a few years ago there was a fish and chip shop here, selling the catch from the boats that operated from the wharf on the inlet; these days the catch is too small, the prices too high, so they buy burgers from the takeaway and settle down at the plastic tables by the car park.

As they eat, Maddie probes Summer about school and friends, careful not to look surprised or frustrated by Summer's studied evasions. Next to her, Ellie looks on without speaking, her face troubled, and not for the first time since they arrived Maddie wonders whether there are things Ellie is not telling her about Summer. Yet when Summer excuses herself to go to the toilet it is Ellie who speaks, turning to Maddie to ask her whether she means to stay on at the beach house.

'Why do you ask?' she says.

'I'm worried about you. Alone down here.'

'I could say the same about you. Up there.'

'That's different,' Ellie says.

'How is it different?'

'Please,' she says, 'you know what I mean.'

Maddie regards her stepdaughter with a steady gaze. Then looks away.

The first year with Declan was revelatory. She loved him with a passion that once would have frightened her. Despite being premature, he slept and fed easily, and even when he didn't she felt buoyed by her feelings for him. She spent whole days marvelling at the fact of him, the movement of his limbs, his delighted, watchful fascination with the world around him. Tom loved him as well, and her the more for having him, the knowledge of their mutual adoration expanding their happiness in a way she never could have predicted.

Absorbed in Declan they let their friends slide, instead spending more and more time down here alone. That was the year the real disasters began – mega-blizzards in North America, tornados in China, the first widespread methane ruptures in Siberia – and it seemed natural to try to shut them out, to concentrate on the fact that here and now they were safe, and had each other.

When Declan turned one they asked a handful of friends to their house in Bondi for a party. Ellie and Adam came, although they were only half together by then. Declan had been walking for more than a month, and Maddie, watching the way Summer held his hand and led him around the garden, thought this was all she would ever need.

After lunch they agree to spread Tom's ashes the following morning, the decision coming surprisingly easily. Perhaps because of this the rest of the day passes without friction, and that evening Summer is talkative, playfully mocking her mother, her school; making jokes at her father's expense.

Yet despite her humour Maddie cannot help but feel there is an edge to Summer's manner, a sharpness to her judgements that is unsettling. There has always been a ferocity in Summer, a ferocity Maddie knows Ellie fears might turn inward, and listening to her vault from subject to subject she wonders if Ellie is right to be afraid, or whether this is just Summer trying to negotiate the treacherous gap between childhood and adolescence: certainly there are times when Maddie, catching Summer glancing at her mother mid-sentence, seeking her approval, sees with painful clarity the undefended nature of Summer's heart, its shifting vulnerability.

After dessert Summer excuses herself and disappears

to her room again. For a time the two older women sit listening to the sound of her voice as she chats with friends.

'Is she okay?' Maddie asks at last.

Ellie takes a sip of wine. 'I really don't know. She's happy enough at school, I think.'

'But?'

'They seem so closed off, these kids, like they've grown up too fast. It frightens me.'

'Because she might hurt herself?'

'Because I don't know what kind of future there is for her,' she said. 'For any of them.'

Later Maddie would wonder whether, if she had noticed the signs earlier, things might have been different, but at first it didn't occur to her it was anything other than a throat infection. He was lethargic and pale, his temperature spiking now and then. Because he'd just begun childcare he'd had a parade of illnesses already that winter, so she ignored it, letting him stay home with her for a day or two, then sending him back. She had just returned to work herself and was struggling with it: she could not take days off all the time.

A week later, Marina, the administrator of his childcare centre, took her aside when she arrived to pick him up. She remembers being worried that it was something serious, her relief when Marina asked whether she'd thought about taking Declan to the doctor.

'Is his throat hurting again?' she asked, and Marina hesitated. Not for long, but long enough.

'It's probably nothing, but there's a lump. I think you should get a doctor to look at it.'

Lying next to him that night, stroking his hair as he fell asleep, she could not imagine how she had missed it, how his body could have become distorted in this way without her noticing. While the lump was not large – little bigger than a marble – its outline was clearly discernible beneath the skin where his neck met his clavicle. When she touched its surface it felt hard, and he pulled away, though not, she imagined, because it hurt exactly, but because it felt wrong somehow.

He took a long time to fall asleep, and it was almost nine by the time she uncurled him from her and rejoined Tom. He looked stricken, his jaw tight. They had not discussed the lump and what it might mean in front of Declan, their conversation limited to a code of omissions and assumptions.

'I've made an appointment for tomorrow,' Tom said, then hesitated, as if there were more.

'And?'

'I called Nick,' he said eventually, his voice flat.

Nick, an anaesthetist, was Tom's oldest friend. They had shared an apartment while at university.

'What did he say?'

'That it could just be some kind of fatty deposit, or a blocked pore, but we should definitely get it checked out.'

'Did he say anything else?'

'Not really. I think he was being careful not to frighten me.'

When she didn't reply Tom put his hand on her shoulder, but she shrugged it off.

'Don't.'

He looked perplexed. 'Why not?'

'Just don't,' she said.

In that first week they bounced from doctor to doctor, diagnosis to diagnosis. The surgeon was practical, optimistic, the oncologist more vague, telling them the road ahead was likely to be difficult. The review panel was even less conclusive. Every time Maddie and Tom took their place in a consulting room they asked the same questions: could their son be cured? How difficult would the treatment be? What was the chance he might die?

And every time, Maddie found herself parsing their words, searching for a certainty no one seemed able to offer her.

In the end surgery was scheduled for the Friday, with chemo to begin a fortnight later. They had their first fight the day after the dates were settled. Tom had been at work, Maddie at the hospital with Declan, watching as he was ushered from ward to ward, his body probed and jabbed and scanned. At three and a half he couldn't comprehend what all this was about, and every time he looked to her for reassurance she wondered if he could see how frightened she was. She couldn't bear it, couldn't bear that Tom wasn't there, that it was she who had to betray their son like this.

The morning of the operation they woke him early. He was hungry, and confused by his parents' refusal to let him eat he became angry. Maddie tried to comfort him, only to lose her temper herself when he wouldn't calm down, shouting at him that she didn't care if he was hungry, she'd had enough, and then bursting into tears when Declan, frightened by her behaviour, began to cry.

These are the things she remembers:

Declan's body in the hospital bed, his limbs so thin it hurt her to look at them.

The view from the window by his bed, the rows in the garden, the intimacy of their disorder.

The smell of the ward, the way it clung to her.

The way time seemed to stretch out across those months, until every second seemed to fill an hour, a day. A week.

She is not sure when she began to withdraw. It was not that she didn't love him, because she did, more than anything; she would have given her own life, right there, right then, would have done anything if it meant he could live even one more day. Yet somehow it seemed easier, more truthful to accept that he was dying, and that nothing she could do, no gesture, no flamboyant display of grieving, would change that.

Tom didn't understand. She saw it in his eyes every day, in the way he hovered over Declan as if the boy were about to break, in the way he gathered the moments. Sometimes she could almost see him thinking, This is the last time we will be here with him, the last time he will go to the zoo, the last time he will run just like this, and she hated him for it, hated him for the way his weakness infected all of them. One night Tom accused her of being cold, so afraid of losing control she could not let herself feel. Only once, and in anger, but it was enough.

There were people to help them, of course, foundations and volunteers and successions of visitors. And in many ways they were lucky: there were families they came to know while they were on the ward who did not have the luxury of money, haunted-looking fathers who appeared late in the evening or early in the morning, mothers who came from jobs as cleaners or in factories, their faces grey with exhaustion.

Later she read figures about the toll childhood cancer took on careers, but at the time she only saw Tom taking leave and allowing his partners to cover for him.

Some of those families they knew by name, others by sight, fellow travellers in the twilight world of the cancer ward. There was a Somali couple whose daughter had leukaemia, a single mother from Penrith whose handsome thirteen-year-old son's osteosarcoma had returned, a gay couple whose daughter had been diagnosed with a brain tumour. She would watch Tom talking to them, his broad-shouldered frame handsome in his rumpled suit, one of their hands grasped in his, and know he was assuaging his own pain by seeking to understand theirs, his need to connect suddenly ridiculous to her.

In time they realised it was easier not to know too much about the others, so as not to have to register their sudden absence from the ward, their ghostly return with flowers or a gift for the staff. Better, they learned, to remain ignorant.

And all the while she could feel the way life sought to regain its equilibrium. The way ordinary life kept fighting its way in, so that grief was never constant but a series of shocks, each one as new, as raw, as the first. How soon would it take for life to reassert itself afterwards? she caught herself wondering. How long before this unimaginable absence became normal?

Still, it was the final weeks that were the worst. His body so tiny, so frail in the bed, his breathing so weak and shallow that each day it seemed impossible he could go on. She could not bear the thought of no longer having him, yet sometimes, seeing what it cost him to stay, she found herself wishing for the end, even as she knew it meant she would not know how to continue living herself. And then, when it seemed he could last no longer, he went. It happened almost suddenly. He was sleeping, he woke up, he convulsed. His body arched and went rigid and then was utterly still.

* * *

The house is quiet next morning, and at first she assumes she must be the first one up. But as she steps into the kitchen she sees Summer sitting on the edge of the deck, back straight, headphones on, lost in whatever it is she is listening to. At the sound of the door she turns, removes her headphones.

'Couldn't sleep?' Maddie asks.

'Not really.'

'Is your mum still asleep?'

'I suppose so,' Summer says.

Maddie gestures to the deck beside Summer. 'Do you mind if I sit down?'

A shake of her head. 'Of course not.'

Seating herself Maddie arranges her robe around her legs, looks out over the lawn into the trees.

'How're things with you?'

Summer too stares out over the grass. 'Okay, I suppose.'

'But?'

She shrugs. 'Mum's so full of shit.'

Maddie hesitates, suddenly wary of intruding. 'What do you mean?'

'I don't know. She wanted us to come here so we could have time together, but then she just ignores me.'

'Go easy on her, she's had a difficult time. Losing Tom.'

'You lost him too.'

Maddie leans across and pushes a lock of hair off Summer's face. 'He was my husband, not my father. My ex-husband.'

When Summer doesn't reply she says, 'I remember the first time you came here. You played out here for hours. I don't suppose you remember that, do you?'

There is silence, then Summer says, 'No.'

'You were so sweet that day.'

Summer flicks an insect off her leg. 'I didn't think you'd want to see me.'

'What?' Maddie asks. 'Why not?'

Summer glances at Maddie and then away again. 'Because I thought I'd remind you of him.'

Maddie puts her arm around Summer's shoulder. 'No,' she says. 'It's not like that, not ever.'

Even before Declan died they both knew it was over, but in the empty days after his funeral neither seemed able to acknowledge it. Although they shared the same house they moved through it separately, barely noticing each other's presence. Weeks before, when they were doing shifts at the hospital, Tom had begun sleeping in the spare room; with Declan gone he showed no sign of coming back.

She knew Tom was suffering as well but she didn't care. She could not imagine his hands on her, could hardly bear the thought of having him near her. She had heard people talk about grief in terms of confusion, but that was not what it was like for her; instead she felt as if she were disappearing, as if everything had been stripped away and all that was left was a space where she had been.

One night a week after Declan's death, Tom came to her bed, appearing in the doorway in the small hours of the morning. She did not speak as he crossed the room and lay beside her, but neither did she resist when he drew her close. In the darkness his body could have been anybody's, and as they moved together she felt as if she might erase herself in the act. Afterwards she knew he was waiting for her to speak, to offer him some sign that they might find their way back to each other, but she said nothing.

He kept the house in Bondi, she took this one. Money too, though not much. For a time she thought she would try to go back to work. But in the end she found it easier to just retreat here, to hide.

It is almost eight before they head down to the bay, the morning air already thick with the scent of approaching heat. The beach is quiet, and save for a small group on the far side they have the sand to themselves.

They choose a spot in the middle of the bay, wading out until the water is up to their knees. Taking the urn from beneath her arm Ellie turns to Maddie and Summer.

'Shall we begin?' she asks.

Maddie looks to Summer for her approval, then nods.

Without speaking Ellie unscrews the urn and shakes a handful of the contents into Maddie's and Summer's hands, careful to avoid spilling any. The ash is so fine, so light it seems barely heavier than air, and as Maddie lifts her hand it seems impossible that this could be all that is left of Tom, that the familiar weight of his body, his presence, should have disappeared so completely. How can that be? she wonders. How can we just pass away, all that we are lost to the air? And then it isn't Tom she is thinking of, but Declan, and that other morning five years ago when she and Tom brought his ashes here and spread them. It had been hot that morning as well, the air shimmering with UV, and Tom had wept but she had barely registered it.

Next to her, Ellie and Summer are crying, tears streaming down their faces, and although she knows she should be as well, she cannot, is held back by the knowledge that if she lets go she will never be able to stop. Ellie turns, a look of reproach on her face, and before Maddie can explain that Ellie has misunderstood, that it is not a lack of love that keeps her from crying but a surfeit of it, her stepdaughter has turned away, one arm extended to draw Summer close, the two of them standing staring out to sea.

As Ellie loads the car Maddie watches, aware that this is the moment she should speak out, stop her going. And yet she does not. This is how it will be now, she sees that; with Tom gone, whatever tenuous bond there was between them is also gone. Only after they have driven off does she know what she should have said.

Back inside she tidies the last of the lunch things, aware of the movement of the light through the trees outside. The last time Tom came up here he stood on the deck and watched the birds. He looked old, his face haggard.

'They're dying, you know,' he said, glancing at her as he spoke.

He waited for her to answer and when she did not he said, 'Not just here but all over the world.'

'They look fine to me,' she said, irritated.

'They might look fine but they've stopped breeding, or if they're still breeding their eggs aren't hatching, or the heat is killing the chicks. The ones you can see here are adults because they're all that's left, and when they're gone that will be the end of them. They're a ghost species.'

'Get out,' she said. 'I don't want you here.'

Remembering that day, she wonders whether it might have been different if she'd tried harder. Perhaps there was some affection left, a tenderness the two of them could have saved. Perhaps if they had, Tom might not have gotten sick.

Through the window she can see the sky, the haze of red already visible. On the outside table a currawong moves, black and fast as a blade. As if sensing her it turns, and its great yellow eye momentarily meets hers, filling her with a sense of its presence, its perturbation of the universe. Tom never liked the currawongs: they were killers, he said, things that preyed on the eggs of other birds. And yet she does not see a killer, she sees something that is simply itself, a logic translated through space. In a moment it will be gone, rising into the sky on stealthy wing beats. And she will be here, alone.

BREAKING
AND
ENTERING

In the evenings, when the bars are closing and there seems to be nowhere else to go, Summer and Meera and Dan slip out into the streets and lanes in search of apartments or houses left vacant for a night or a week or a month. Sometimes they buzz the neighbours, apologising for the hour as they tell them they're from next door and they've forgotten their key, sometimes they just linger near the entrance, emerging at the last moment to slip through the door behind homecoming couples. If anybody asks questions Meera smiles and looks into their eyes and says, 'We just moved in last weekend,' or, 'Didn't you know? We're minding the place for my parents,' and usually they smile back because she's beautiful and they want her. Other times they clamber over fences, or dodge along car-park ramps as the gates roll down, laughing and shouting, their footsteps echoing off the concrete walls.

There are cameras, of course, but there are cameras everywhere, and the danger is part of why they do it. Sometimes as they're stumbling into a lift or racing through a car park she will catch a glimpse of Dan's face, see the way he is riding the thrill of it, his eyes alight, and the knowledge she is here with him will make her feel giddy, electric, the feeling so intense she can barely speak.

The first time, it almost seemed to happen by accident. It was November, the weekend after exams ended, and they had been out celebrating, first at a party in Newtown and then a series of bars in Redfern. But when the last bar closed and none of them could decide what to do they ended up out in the street, running and laughing, their senses alive in the warm embrace of the night. Eventually she stopped and asked where they should go next.

'There has to be somewhere,' Dan said, and turned expectantly to Meera, who was staring back up the street as if searching for something in the distance. She seemed to shine, her dark eyes liquid.

'We could go to Anouk's house,' she said.

'Anouk's away,' Summer said.

'So?' Meera said. 'I know her parents' security code, she told me last time I was there.'

Next to her Dan was grinning. 'Anouk's got a pool,' he

said, and Summer shivered, feeling as if the two of them were leaving her behind.

Anouk's father was some sort of banker, and although he'd lost a lot in the crash the house had been bought before things really went bad. Once they were through the gates they stripped off and jumped into the pool, its blue-lit water warm and salty as blood.

They had pills with them that night but didn't take them. Instead they floated, staring up at the night sky and talking, listening to the chitter of the bats and the distant rumble of the traffic, then wandered through the darkened house, exploring the rooms one by one. At one point Summer found Meera in the master bedroom going through Anouk's mother's clothes. They were beautiful, expensive, flowing things, in silky fabrics and elegant cuts. Seeing Summer standing in the doorway, Meera threw her a dress and stood waiting, her chin lifted in silent challenge, until Summer reached down and peeled off her top to try it on.

A week later they broke into the house of a friend of Dan's whose parents were in Bali. There was no pool this time so they danced and drank and rifled through the house, until finally the sky grew pale and they went out into the grey of the dawn and dove into the waves at Bondi. The next time it was the house of a friend of Meera's father, the time after that an apartment left empty when its new owners' finance fell through, which Dan had heard about through a friend of his uncle's.

Sometimes when she is alone she tries to understand why they keep doing it. There is the excitement, of course, the fear of getting caught, the elation when they are not. Yet there is something in the way Meera takes possession of the houses, the casual manner in which she rips and destroys and invades privacies, that suggests it is about more than that, at least for her – it's as if their intrusions are less about the risk than about transgression, power.

One night, high on ecstasy, Meera kisses her, open-mouthed, and closing her eyes Summer dissolves into the moment, the embrace, the cool presence of Meera's flesh.

She is not certain now whether this is how she wanted it to be. Her and Meera and Dan, her and Dan and Meera, Meera and Dan and her. A year ago they barely knew each other, were just faces across the yard at school, then one day she turned around to find Meera standing beside her.

'Are you coming on Saturday night?' she asked.

Summer was so surprised it took her a few seconds to reply.

'You mean to Scarlett's?'

Meera looked at her as if the question were ridiculous.

'Sure,' Summer said. 'I suppose,' aware as she spoke of the way Meera held her gaze a fraction too long, the casual way she nodded and turned away.

She hadn't really been planning to go. She'd been asked, they all had, but most of her friends had already agreed the party wasn't for them. But when Sophie came over a moment later and asked what Meera had wanted Summer just shrugged and said it was nothing.

Meera didn't speak to her again that week, and when Saturday night arrived Summer zipped herself into the dress she'd bought to wear to Sophie's birthday. She was at her dad's, which was good, since he asked fewer questions.

'You're going out?' he said when she appeared in the living room at nine o'clock.

'Just for a while,' she said.

'Who with?'

She wasn't sure why she was uncomfortable with the question. 'Just Sophie and some of the others,' she said, the lie coming with surprising fluidity.

He looked at her thoughtfully. 'You be careful.'

'Of course,' she said.

Scarlett lived in Glebe, in a big house near the water. By

the time Summer arrived the place was already full, people crammed into the rooms and hall. There were faces she knew here and there but many more she didn't, and as she made her way through the crowd she willed herself to be cool, not to smile too hard or panic.

She found Meera dancing with a group of guys in the backyard. Unwilling to interrupt, reluctant to head back inside, she hovered on the edge of the dance floor, until finally Meera noticed her and dived across to draw her close.

'Are you having fun?' she shouted over the music, her mouth pressed to Summer's ear. Summer laughed and began to say she'd only just got there, but Meera was already pulling her on, towards the back fence where Dan was talking to a couple of guys Summer knew from school.

As they drew level with him Dan turned and smiled. Later she would realise he was already high, but that night all she felt was the force of his attention.

'This is Summer,' Meera said, and he grinned again, pushing his hair out of his eyes with one hand.

'From school, right?' he asked.

Summer nodded, but before Dan could say anything else the music changed and Meera took their arms and dragged them onto the dance floor, saying, 'I love this song, come dance with me.'

Her dad was still up when she got home.

'You're late,' he said when she appeared flushed and sweaty at the door, but she just shrugged and told him she couldn't find a cab.

Later she wondered why Meera had wanted her there, what she wanted *from* her, but that night, sprawled on her bed alone in her room, she seemed to float, eyes closed, skin damp and thrillingly alive.

Summer is thinking about that night when Meera pings her and says she and Dan are at Interstice, in Redfern. It embarrasses her, the way she feels herself start into life when she reads the message. Excited and nervous, her legs trembling beneath her, she stands to dress.

The band are called The Mirrors. Two men and three women with matching platinum-blond hair dressed in tight, shiny silver suits that make them look like creatures from a planet where the New Wave never ended. Their music is sexy and infectious, little compressions of sweetness and purity about love and desire played fast and hard.

Meera knows the guy on keyboards and afterwards they go backstage. When they played the band had seemed ice-cool and aloof, faces unreadable behind dark glasses, but in the green room they joke and laugh, high on the thrill of the show.

And then it is happening. One minute they are drinking and laughing and then all of a sudden the place is closing and they are outside. It is two a.m., too early to go home, so when Meera says she knows a place in Darling Point nobody disagrees.

The band have a van, so they bundle in the back with the gear from the show, the electric engine straining as they speed away through the streets. In the darkness Meera slips a pill into Summer's mouth, and she throws her head back and swallows. The air is warm, heavy with the smell of smoke from the fires that have been burning on the city's fringes for the past week.

Outside the building Meera tells the others to wait, then borrowing the band's blond wigs, the three of them bundle in through the lobby and into the lifts, moving fast to avoid the cameras. Meera instructs the lights to come on and a warm glow fills the space while Dan looks for the sound system. A moment later music is playing, a song Summer recognises at once, and loves. Catching her delight, Dan smiles back and she feels like she will burst.

Then the others are there, not just the band but a collection of people they seem to have picked up along the way, faces Summer doesn't know. Some dance, others hunt through the kitchen in search of alcohol. Buoyed, Summer stumbles out onto the balcony.

She feels weightless, suspended in the timelessness of the darkness. On the other side of the harbour lights are visible, the sky is purple. Closing her eyes she grips the rail tighter, feeling the chemicals course through her blood.

And then a voice, a body, next to her. Dan's.

'Hey,' she says.

'You good?' he asks.

'Great,' she says.

'You can see the fires,' Dan says, pointing at the glow along the horizon.

'They're beautiful, aren't they?'

She wants to touch him. 'Dan?' she asks, and he looks at her.

'Summer?' he says, his voice teasing but friendly.

'Have you and Meera ever . . .?'

He grins. 'Ever what?'

'You know.'

He looks away again, his eyes focusing on the far side of the harbour. 'No.'

'Not ever?'

He laughs. 'Why do you want to know?'

* * *

Looking back on that moment in the days and weeks to come she will wonder whether Dan just didn't understand the question or whether he chose to ignore it. Perhaps he was lying, perhaps he was stoned, perhaps both of them were in love with Meera. For now, though, she simply goes back inside.

The music has grown louder but Meera isn't in the living room. Summer finds her seated on the bed in the master bedroom, a pair of lenses in her hand.

'Look at the playlist,' Meera says, beckoning her across and slipping the lenses over her eyes.

The lenses are new, expensive, but the system is easy enough to navigate. Flicking through the menu Summer calls up the playlist, discovers an inventory of what looks like porn. As always when confronted with these sorts of images in company she feels disquiet, a charged field of uncertainty about how to react.

'Notice anything?' Meera asks.

Summer is about to say no when she catches her breath. 'It's all gay.'

Meera laughs. 'No wonder his wife left him.'

Summer shifts a little, aware of Meera's body against hers.

'You think that was why?'

Meera's breath is warm against Summer's neck. 'Try opening the bedroom system.'

Pulling up the link, Summer activates it. Suddenly she is looking at herself and Meera seated on the bed.

'There's a camera!'

'There are four,' Meera says, and as she speaks Summer realises there are, each showing the bed from a different angle.

'Now look at the recordings.'

Returning to the playlist, Summer opens the first file and the room around her fills with holos of men gripping and coupling. For fifteen, maybe twenty seconds she watches the bodies move against each other, then she takes the lenses off.

Meera is regarding her with amusement. 'Well?' she asks.

Summer shakes her head. A few seconds ago she wanted to tell Meera how close she'd felt to Dan out on the balcony. But now all she can see is the pleasure Meera is taking in this evidence of a secret life, and in Summer's discomfort with it. 'We shouldn't be doing this,' she says.

'Why not? He won't know.'

'That doesn't matter,' she says, pressing the lenses back into Meera's hand. 'It's still private.'

Meera laughs. 'When did you get so uptight?'

'I'm not uptight, I just think this is wrong.' She stands.

Meera is still smiling but her eyes are cold.

'If you want to keep looking, feel free.'

Dan is nowhere to be seen when she gets back to the living room, so pushing her way past the dancers she goes through to the kitchen. In here it is bright, the lights forming pools upon the gleaming bench tops. In the corner one of the boys is seated next to the sink with his back against the splashback, the drummer leaning into him, their eyes closed and mouths pressed together, both so lost in the moment they do not register her presence.

She should leave, take her bag and walk out into the night, but she is not quite ready for that yet, not quite ready to let go. Picking up a bottle of beer she raises it to her lips, the sharp taste of it filling her mouth as the cool liquid runs down her throat.

Before she met Meera she and her friends were always involved in whatever cause was most urgent. Along with Sophie she helped raise money for refugees, joined the marches and occupations, even spent some time on one of the coalmine blockades. But Meera and

Dan don't care about politics: Meera in particular goes out of her way to show her contempt for people who make the mistake of caring, her disdain so keen Summer sometimes wonders how much of it is directed at her. Looking at the scene around her, she remembers that other version of herself, the thought of what she has become making her feel ill, a revulsion so overwhelming she can barely keep it in.

In the next room somebody is playing a song from the summer before, a shrieking, whirling shiver of a tune. Setting her bottle down she heads back through, closing her eyes as she steps into the beat, letting it lift her, carry her, losing herself amongst the bodies of the others.

When the song ends it is replaced by another, and then another, each one leading her on into the next, until at last she turns to see Dan standing by the door, Meera beside him. They are talking, their arms wound around each other, Dan explaining something with the intentness that she loves. Without thinking she stops moving, her arms falling to her side, and as she does Meera looks around, her eyes meeting Summer's. For a split second Meera seems caught off guard but then she smiles, and Summer is reminded of the look on her face that first night in Anouk's mother's bedroom as she went through the woman's things, the way she revelled in that power. Pushing her way past the others she walks back to the balcony, steps out into the warm dark. Gripping the rail she looks northward towards the glow of the fires, closes her eyes, breathes in the smoky air.

BOILING THE FROG

'Home?' the woman beside Adam asks as the plane banks towards its final approach.

Looking across, he shakes his head. 'No,' he says. 'Just visiting.'

The woman smiles. She has spent most of the flight asleep or with lenses on. She is younger than he is, neatly blonde with the look of the professional business traveller.

'Work or family?' she asks, and now Adam can hear that she is not Australian or English, but South African.

'Work. A conference,' he says, unwilling to go into more detail.

Whatever she is about to say next is cut off by the steward telling them they have landed. Adam straightens, happy to break off the conversation.

In the terminal it is busy. All week the Met Office and NASA have been tracking a tropical hurricane in the

Atlantic, a monster called Medea, as it moves eastwards and north, sending fronts ahead of itself. Tropical storms have struck England more than once in recent years, yet if the simulations are correct Medea will be bigger than anything that has struck before, and there are reports of impending airport closures, a constant press of travellers eager to get out while they can. On the concourse crowds wait, families of Indians and Pakistanis surrounded by small mountains of hand luggage, lone travellers slumped half asleep, couples and families absorbed in their screens and overlays, lost in some shared solitude. Near the escalators to the baggage claim Adam passes a harried-looking mother with three small children dragging behind her and another in her arms, registers the look of exhaustion in her eyes.

When he eventually finds his way to the station under the terminal, the platform is packed, and the train, when it arrives, crowded and slow, its journey interrupted by a series of unexplained delays, long periods of idling in stations and tunnels. Despite the forecast the morning is clear, but as he emerges from the Tube it is difficult to believe things are as they should be. Although it is barely eight the morning already shimmers with heat, and there is a foulness in the air, a stink of drains and humidity he more readily associates with the tropics than with England's south-east.

In his hotel room he drops his bags and slumps down on the bed. Dislocated by the movement across time zones his body is heavy with exhaustion yet restless and unsettled, and as he lies back he feels the contradictory pull of the desire to sleep and a nervous, unnatural wakefulness; rousing himself, he turns on the shower and steps under the water, his skin crawling as if with fever.

As he dresses he flicks through the conference information in his overlays. Amidst it he notices the advice to wear insect repellent at dusk and dawn in order to stave off the possibility of drug-resistant malaria; wondering how real the risk is, he makes a mental note to read the figures.

Once he is done he turns his overlays off and begins to transfer the things he will need from his suitcase to his backpack. He has plans for the two days between now and the opening address, plans of a more personal nature. Yet now that the time has come for them he is afraid, not of what he will find but of what might follow.

It was her friend Sophie who gave him the address. When they spoke she was evasive, leaving him uncertain whether she was in contact with Summer or not. Back in Sydney he'd called up a satellite image of the house, which was outside a small town in Norfolk, realising as it appeared on his screen that he was trembling, the possibility that he might glimpse her in it almost overwhelming, a sensation that was replaced by emptiness when all he saw was a stone cottage, broken plastic toys scattered in front of it.

Heading out into the street he feels a shadow of that feeling return, but as he turns towards Kings Cross he does his best to put it aside, to concentrate instead on his determination to find her.

In the time he has been inside the air has grown even hotter, although the blue sky is now marked by ribs of cloud feeding in from the south-west. Yet the weather is less striking than the changes to the city in the decade since he was last here – the closed shops, the beggars sleeping on footpaths, the cracks in the asphalt, the groups of young people congregated on corners. The police vans with blackened windows parked every block or two.

On the train he takes a seat by the window. The timetable says the trip should take slightly over an hour and a half, but even before they reach the edge of the city it is clear they will be late. Ordinarily this would be a source of frustration, but today he finds he is grateful for the chance to lose himself in observation of the passing countryside, struck all over again by the sheer bounty of the English summer, the pressing green and life, so unexpected in the midst of so much change.

In Cambridge he collects a car and settles back as it winds its way towards the city's fringes. In the lanes heading west, cars are queued in long lines. Some of the waiting vehicles seem to be ordinary traffic, but many are packed with bags and children, or are pulling trailers, the effect more reminiscent of the first day of holidays than the evacuation it clearly is. Yet while the traffic heading west is heavy, for the most part the road to the east is clear, and as he leaves the city behind he allows the car to accelerate into the countryside.

As a student he spent a summer living in England, and travelled this way more than once. Back then the flat fields and rows of hedges and houses always seemed like a reminder of another age, unaltered by the passage of time. Even now much is the same, yet it is difficult to ignore the stands of genetically engineered trees that line the edges of fields, unnaturally tall against the remaining clumps of oak and pine. The most visible of the various organisms developed in the last decade or so to consume and store carbon dioxide, they have come to be known as triffids, a name that captures the unsettlingly alien blurring of plant and flesh suggested by their thick boles and distorted dimensions. But to Adam's eyes what their smooth, slightly bulbous trunks and inverted canopies most resemble is the great baobabs that once grew in Madagascar.

When they were first developed many assumed the motivation was financial rather than ecological, citing as evidence the decision of the companies that created them to patent their genomes instead of making them available for free. Environmental groups fought their introduction hard, poisoning fields earmarked for their planting and burning plantations, but governments here and elsewhere held firm, arguing that the importance of capturing carbon dioxide far outweighed the risk of further contamination of the ecosystem.

Unsurprisingly these assurances soon proved incorrect. Only months after the first plantations were established, triffids had begun to turn up along waterways and in forests across England and Scotland, a process that was repeated in other countries, one more factor in the ongoing transformation of the world's ecosystems.

When he was younger he would have been on the side of the protesters, would have regarded the intrusion of these unnatural tropical creations into this landscape as a catastrophe. But looking at them now he finds himself wondering if they are not simply the latest stage in a process that goes back millennia. After all, these fields were once wetlands, a vast interconnected maze of low pools and streams and marshes stretching from Cambridge to the sea. Then, two hundred years ago, humans drained the land, constructing embankments and pumping the water out to sea to create space for farms and roads and forests. With the water gone the land changed. Fishing and fowling gave way to farming, farms to factories. Even the birds that congregated here began to disappear, some dying, others finding new breeding grounds, altering their migratory routes. And in their place the land itself took on new shapes.

Some of those shapes can still be seen, records of the area's long occupation, as are the birds that move overhead, or stand in the pools and streams beside the road.

Now, though, the sea is returning. In recent years these fields and towns have flooded more than once, and although the windmills that drive the drainage systems testify to people's determination to keep the water at bay, it is really only a way of delaying the inevitable.

Those who live here know this, of course. Hence the signs of preparation, the rowboats on trailers in driveways and on lawns, the canoes and kayaks propped against walls.

There was a time when people talked about boiling the frog, arguing that the warming of the planet was too gradual to galvanise effective action, and although in recent years that has changed, delay having been replaced by panic, resistance by calls for more effective solutions, Adam still suspects that at some level people do not understand the scale of the transformation that is overtaking them. Even if it hasn't happened yet, the reality is that this place is already lost, that some time soon the ocean will have it back, the planet will overwhelm it.

Half an hour outside Cambridge the car interrupts to alert him to the turn-off, its driving system steering smoothly to the right. The wheels crunch as they hit gravel and then bump onto dirt.

The drive is long and narrow, a straight muddy track fenced in on both sides by low hedges. At its end an ancient yew tree stands, its spreading canopy shading an old gate held in place by pillars of stone. Directing the car to park, Adam opens the door and steps out into the glare of the heat.

Beyond the gate the path continues past a disused well to an old farmhouse. Georgian, he thinks, looking up at the high windows and steep roof. Once it would have been the only building, now other structures rise behind it: a barn, two small wind turbines, and further off to the north what looks to be some kind of accommodation block built out of second-hand bricks and metal cladding.

At the front door he rings the bell. On the step a child's tri-cycle lies overturned, a half-deflated ball beside it; from within he can hear children's voices. After a few moments a woman opens the door and peers at him with thinly disguised hostility. A few years younger than Adam, she wears a shapeless, dowdy dress, her hair pulled back unflatteringly from her broad face.

Smiling hopefully he tells her he is looking for Summer.

'Summer who?' she asks suspiciously.

'Summer Leith.'

'And you are?'

'Adam Leith. Her father.'

Somewhere behind her a child cries out, but she does not turn around.

'Where did you get this address?'

'From a friend of Summer's back in Australia. She doesn't know I'm coming.'

The screaming has grown louder. The woman glances over her shoulder, then turns back to him. 'Wait here,' she says.

He stands on the doorstep listening to her separating the children, her voice raised in a high, falsely cheery tone at odds with her manner a moment before. Once order has been restored there is a silence, then her voice again, lower and more cautious this time, the tone and the gaps between speech telling him she is on the phone. Quite suddenly he feels himself begin to tremble, all the nervousness of recent days descending upon him.

Then she reappears in the narrow hall. He tries to look casual as she fixes him with a cold stare.

'She said you should go up.'

The woman directs him to a track he had not noticed before. Like the drive he came in on, it is bordered by low stone walls built centuries before, and runs off across the fields. A kilometre or so further on it terminates near a clump of trees and another house.

'I can drive?'

She glances at his car with distaste. 'I suppose,' she says.

Although the track is bad the drive takes only a few minutes. Near the house he sees a figure standing in the doorway and knows immediately it is her. Unsure now of how to proceed he pulls the car in, gets out.

It is close to a decade since she left for England, and almost as long since he saw her in person, but from a distance she looks little different, the way she stands, arms folded, head cocked to one side, immediately, achingly familiar.

She does not speak as he approaches. The yard is a ruin, the grass flattened and muddy. He stops a little way in front of her.

'Summer.' After so long it is all he can manage.

'Dad.'

'I'm sorry to just appear like this.'

'Is something wrong? Is Mum . . .?'

'No, no, nothing like that.'

He wants to step forward, take her in his arms, but he is afraid she will push him away.

Finally she steps aside. 'Would you like to come in?' she says.

The house is cluttered and dirty and smells of mildew. Although somebody has made an attempt to brighten the place by spreading coloured cloths over the sofas and positioning rag rugs in the doorways, these decorations cannot disguise the fact that the furniture is cheap and broken, or distract from the tide mark that runs along the walls at chest height.

At the end of the hall she ushers him into the kitchen,

where a man is seated at the table, a screen in front of him. He is thirtyish, dark-haired with a wispy beard, and as they enter he looks up, nods without warmth. Glancing at Summer, Adam waits for her to introduce him but she does not. Instead she studiously ignores the man's presence.

'Would you like a drink?'

'That would be lovely,' he says.

While she pours him a glass of water he studies the room, taking in the chipped plates on the draining board, the cluttered benches. The man at the table continues to study his screen as if Adam and Summer are not there, the effect disconcerting in such a small space. Only as they are leaving does he look up again, his eyes settling coldly on Adam.

Outside Summer motions to him to sit, then perches on a broken chair opposite. The air swells with the sound of insects, the massing shapes of gnats and dragonflies. On the far side of the yard a rusted trampoline hangs twisted in the boughs of a tree.

Catching him looking at it she says, 'Last summer.'

'Did you lose much?'

'Stuff? Some. But people died, Dad. A lot of them. Or had you forgotten that?'

'Of course not.'

She seems to be considering whether to push the point.

But then, for whatever reason, she relaxes.

'I'm sorry,' she says. 'I'm just worried about the storm.'

'Everybody is.'

'Is that why you're here?'

'In England? No, I'm here for a conference. Adaptation strategies.'

'And you thought you'd look me up?'

'I wanted to see you. It's been a long time.'

Again he sees the way she moves almost to the point of confrontation and then backs away.

'Yes,' she says. 'It has.'

'What is this place?'

'What do you mean?'

'I mean, is it your house? From what Sophie said it sounded like some kind of community, or commune.'

'It's just a house, Dad.'

He nods, fighting not to respond. 'And that man in the kitchen?'

She glances back at the house. 'Neil? He rents one of the rooms.'

'So you're not . . .?'

She looks at him incredulously, then laughs, suddenly her younger self again. 'With that prick? Jesus, Dad!'

Adam smiles, relieved. 'What about the woman at the

main house, the one who sent me here?'

'Adeline? She's been here a long while.'

He takes a sip of his water, stares out over the landscape. 'It can't be easy living here.'

'It's not. But it's cheap.'

'There must be other places that are cheap?'

She shakes her head in exasperation. 'If you must know, it was a cooperative, but it dissolved after the last round of floods. Now we're just squatting.'

'I'm sorry,' he says, 'I didn't mean to pry.'

'I'm not political any more, if that's what you're asking.'

He remembers how easily she used to be able to throw him off balance, how impossible he found it to steel himself against it.

'It wasn't.'

She takes a breath, and when she speaks again her voice is calmer. 'I'm sorry. It's just, this is difficult.'

'I know,' he begins, 'I'm sorry —' but before he can continue he becomes aware of a presence behind him, and turns to find a boy standing in the doorway. Seven, maybe eight, dark skin, almond-shaped eyes, his body tensed. He shoots Adam a quick look, his gaze skittering away almost immediately.

'Mum?' he says, one finger tapping an agitated rhythm

on the side of his leg. For several seconds there is silence. Then Summer glances at Adam.

'This is Noah,' she says.

Adam doesn't move. He knows he should speak but he cannot find the words, and in the end it is Summer who breaks the awkwardness.

'What is it, Noah?'

'There's people on the feeds saying the storm's changing course.'

Summer gets up and goes over to him. 'I know,' she says. 'I saw.'

'Should we leave?'

'Not yet.'

'Are you sure?'

'Quite sure.'

'Should we ask Adeline?'

'No.'

'Are you *really* sure?'

There is something odd about the way the boy holds himself, and about the thinness of his arms and legs protruding from his shorts and T-shirt.

'Shall I get my stuff?'

'Okay,' Summer says exhaustedly, then rights herself. 'Wait. Noah, this is Adam.'

The boy doesn't look at him, just shifts uncomfortably from foot to foot.

'Your grandfather.'

Adam feels something dislocate within. He looks at Summer and then back to Noah. The boy twists sideways, then as if deciding he has waited long enough darts back inside.

'Why didn't you tell me?' Adam asks. His hands are trembling.

Summer looks at him, and for a moment he sees her as the child she once was, fierce yet frighteningly vulnerable. She shakes her head.

'Not now,' she says.

Adam waits but she doesn't continue.

'You're alone here with him?' he asks at last, his voice quiet.

'I am.'

'And his father?'

Summer looks away. 'Gone.'

'And Noah is the reason you haven't come home?'

'Partly.' Adam can see his daughter's old defences coming down, see her looking for some edge of disapproval to latch onto. Determined not to give it to her he says slowly, 'But he's worried about the storm.'

'It's more than that. He's obsessed with it, with the reports.'

'I'm not surprised. It must be frightening for him.'

'No,' she says. 'It's not just that.'

Her tone makes Adam pause. 'What do you mean?'

'He's on the spectrum.'

Adam fumbles for a response. 'How badly?' he eventually asks.

'High-functioning. But all this stuff, with the water and the flood and the storm, it stresses him, makes him worse. He gets incredibly wound-up, can't stop talking about it.'

Adam extends a hand, takes hers in his. 'Summer,' he says at last, 'I'm sorry.'

She pulls away. 'We need to go see about the storm,' she says.

Noah is seated on the sofa, hunched over a screen. Kneeling down, Summer takes it from him and reads it for a few seconds.

'He's right. It's changed course again. I think we need to go.'

'Go where?' Adam asks.

'There's an evac centre in Norwich,' she says, her voice uncertain.

'But?'

'The last storm hit Norwich hard. Things are still pretty rough over there.'

'I've got a hotel room in London. You could come there.'

'It's a long way.'

'At least it'll be safe.' As Adam speaks he sees that Neil has appeared in the doorway.

'You'd be safer heading for Norwich with me and Adeline and the others.'

Summer gives Neil a look of ill-concealed dislike. 'No,' she says. 'We'll go to London.'

Neil turns to Adam. 'What if they've closed the roads?'

Irritated by the younger man's assumption that he will find an ally in him, Adam shakes his head. 'It's Summer's call.'

Neil's expression turns cold. 'Fine,' he says. 'Can you at least drop me at Adeline's?'

Adam glances at Summer, who gives a quick nod. 'Sure,' he says. 'As long as you're ready.'

Summer and Noah have bags packed in anticipation of leaving, but when Adam returns from loading them into the car he finds her moving from room to room locking windows and bolting doors.

'There'll be looters,' she says. 'Although I don't think

we'll be back anyway. Not this time.'

They drop Neil at the main house, then drive on towards the road. Adam leaves the car on auto and turns to Noah, who is clutching his screen in the back seat.

'What do the reports say now?'

The boy ignores the question and draws his shoulders in tighter.

Adam tries a different tack. 'Have you been to London before?'

Noah begins poking at his screen with a rapid motion clearly designed to shut Adam out.

'Noah,' Summer says, her tone weary, mechanical, as if this reprimand has been issued many times.

'Once,' the boy says without looking up.

When he doesn't elaborate she looks at Adam. 'To see a specialist,' she says.

Once they are back on the main road the traffic quickly grows heavier, pushing forward in fits and starts. Outside Swaffham it finally comes to a halt. The heat is oppressive now, and while the sky is still clear a thunderhead is rising to the west. Glancing over his shoulder, Adam catches Summer's eye, knows she has seen it too.

Beside her Noah stares out across the fields, counting soundlessly as the landscape moves by. Although the situation still feels unreal, Adam's shock is slowly wearing off, to be replaced by an echoing sense of the insuperability of the distance Summer has placed between the two of them.

Yet despite his confusion there is also a part of him that is not surprised. For all that he loves her there was always something self-abnegating in Summer's nature, a tendency to wall herself off from others, to refuse assistance, that only grew more pronounced as she got older.

But where had this tendency come from? In his darker moments he used to blame himself and Ellie, the messy nature of their final years together and eventual separation. He has read studies suggesting that the presence in early childhood of high levels of the chemicals associated with stress can alter the brain's chemistry for life, making children more prone to depression, reducing their impulse control. Looking at her now, sitting with Noah in the seat behind him, he feels the prick of that guilt again.

They are outside Cambridge when the traffic grinds to a halt once more. This time it is not a jam but a roadblock, maintained by green-clad soldiers and a pair of armoured vehicles. Climbing out, Adam is surprised to see Summer open the door behind him. Noah is still glued to his screen.

'He'll be fine,' she says.

They make their way along the line of parked cars. To the south and west the clouds have grown heavier, a great mass of darkness filling half the sky, and the air is thick with humidity. At the barrier a crowd of thirty or forty has gathered, its mood tense. A pair of young men and an older woman are arguing with one of the soldiers.

'What's going on?' Adam asks a man standing nearby.

'They're saying we need to go back to Norwich because the evac centre in Cambridge is full.'

'But that's insane,' Summer says, stepping forward. 'The feeds say Norwich is full as well.'

The man looks her up and down. 'I'm not the one you have to convince.'

'What about people bound for London? Are they letting them through?'

The man jerks his head towards the barrier. 'Is there something wrong with your ears? The road's closed.'

In front of them the taller of the young men pressed against the barrier shouts, and lifting a finger jabs the soldier he's been arguing with in the chest. Two of the other soldiers take a step forward.

Adam grabs his daughter's arm. 'Let's go,' he says, but she is already backing away.

At the car they lean close. 'What are we going to do?' Adam asks, glancing along the line of vehicles.

'I don't know. We can't go back.'

Adam looks up. The heat has reached a new crescendo and the cloud is beginning to blot out the sun. In the distance there is a rumble of thunder.

'We need to get inside,' he says. 'And soon.'

Summer stares at the people standing by their cars or seated on the verge fanning themselves. Lifting a hand to shade her eyes she looks out across the fields.

'There,' she says, careful not to point or make her attention too obvious. 'That group of buildings.'

Adam turns to follow her line of sight. 'What if they don't let us in?' Flicking his overlays on he pulls up a map. 'There's some kind of designated shelter about three kilometres ahead. We can walk that in under an hour if we hurry.'

'What about the car?'

As she speaks a gust of wind licks its way through the grass towards them.

'Leave it,' Adam says.

He grabs Summer's bag while she gets Noah out of the car and clips his backpack around him. Then, eyes down and with Noah between them, they walk quickly along the line of cars until it is possible to cross the verge and clamber over the fence. As Adam helps Summer into the field a cry goes up ahead: the crowd is attempting to push past the roadblock, and Adam sees one of the soldiers bring the butt of his rifle down on a woman in a floral dress.

Once they are far enough away from the roadblock they veer back towards the road. The wind is stronger now, the gusts faster, and thunder cracks and rumbles. The sun has disappeared behind the massing darkness of the clouds, and what light is left is weird, greenish; on the far side of the field a stand of trees bends before the wind, limbs dancing and thrashing in a strange, silent motion. Adam measures his pace, trying not to leave Summer and Noah behind, but he keeps having to slow down to let them catch up, willing himself to stay calm as they struggle towards him, until eventually he passes his bag to Summer, grasps Noah under the arms and swings the boy up.

They are still a kilometre from the shelter when the first wave of the storm hits, a wall of rain racing across the fields towards them. Even after a lifetime in Sydney Adam finds the sheer volume of water startling, the way they are drenched almost immediately. Yet it isn't the rain that is truly frightening but the wind, which strikes like a living thing, bending trees back upon themselves and flinging branches and bins and scraps of clothing through the air. In

Adam's arms Noah makes a low, keening noise, clinging to him like an animal.

The rain is so heavy Adam misses the church that has been designated as the shelter, and it is only when Summer grabs his arm and pulls him around that he sees it through the murk. She shouts something at him but her words are swept away, then they are running together, bodies bent over against the force of the storm, up the path to the door.

There are close to a hundred people inside, huddled on camp beds and pews, and while several greet them with cautious nods as they enter, nobody attempts to welcome them, until eventually a woman approaches with a blanket and ushers them to a clear space.

Noah still clings to Adam, his eyes screwed shut. Pressing his face into the boy's head, Adam breathes in the smell of his hair, a cold smell like leaves and forest water. He wraps the blanket around him, then unpicking his fingers, gently passes him to Summer. 'He's cold.'

She folds him in her arms. 'He's safe,' she says. 'Which is what matters.'

As it turns out, that first deluge is only the precursor to the real thing, which strikes in the early evening. At first it seems that the storm is ending, the wind dropping away to leave only the deafening clamour of the rain. But the lull lasts only a few minutes before it returns with a terrifying wailing sound that makes the building shift and pull. On the other side of the hall a baby begins to cry, but otherwise those gathered around them are silent, withdrawn.

There is a primal quality to the sound of the wind, Adam thinks, about the force of the storm in general – he can feel it, an animal dread, deep in his body. With each gust and shake of the building, each groan of the roof, his dread is supplemented by the fear that the structure will give way, exposing them to the elements.

Somewhere after midnight the wind begins to drop once more, its unearthly shriek fading to a low howl and the steady roar of the rain. Having held, the church now seems to move with the wind like a ship on the ocean.

Around them figures lie sleeping or waiting. In another corner the vicar sits with a couple and their three small children, one hand on the woman's shoulder. By the altar a group of young people – students perhaps – are huddled together, screens open in front of them.

On the floor between Adam and Summer, Noah lies curled in on himself, his head on his backpack. Earlier he was dreaming, his lips moving and his body jerking in some inward agitation, but now he is still, mouth slightly open, body loose.

'I'm amazed he can sleep,' Summer says, and Adam glances up and smiles.

'Kids can sleep through anything.'

She gives a soft snort. 'Not Noah. He's never been a sleeper.'

'No?'

'He's better now. When he was a baby it was a disaster. He wouldn't sleep for longer than forty-five minutes until he was fifteen months old, and even then it was only a few hours at a stretch.'

'That must have been difficult.'

She makes a small sound of resignation, and as he had in her garden Adam catches a glimpse of a profound weariness. 'I've sort of given up. These days he just rattles about the house until he falls asleep.'

'What about school?'

'It doesn't seem to affect that.'

Adam shifts so he can look at her more easily. 'How bad is he?'

'At school he's okay. Excellent at maths, good with computers. He has some trouble with language but he reads okay.'

'Is there a prognosis of some kind, an assessment?'

'He's reasonably high-functioning, but he'll never be normal.'

'And at home?'

'You saw.'

'Not really.'

'It's hard. He needs so much looking after.'

'But you're good with him.'

'No,' she says, a tic of anger moving beneath her words. 'No, I'm not. I'm angry with him all the time. I can't help it, I get frustrated – he's frustrating – but I lose it with him and then feel bad because it wasn't his fault. I tell myself I won't do it again but then I do and I feel worse. It's not fair on him, but half the time I don't care.' She takes a deep breath. 'I once read something by a woman who said that the one thing no mother would say was that she wished she hadn't had children, that she would have been better off without them.'

'But?'

'I do wish it. All the time.'

Adam considers extending a hand, taking hers, but her expression warns him not to. 'Why didn't you tell us? We could have helped.'

She glares at him. 'How? By offering me advice and telling me what I'm doing wrong?' She catches herself, and for several seconds the two of them sit in silence. When she continues her voice is quieter, more careful.

'I didn't mean for it to be like this. When I left I needed to believe I could make things different, better somehow, but that didn't work out, and after that things were such a mess that I thought it would be better if I stayed away.'

'Even with Noah?'

Her expression is unreadable. 'Even with Noah.'

Around daybreak the steady roar of the rain on the roof slows, becomes quieter, more random, before finally stopping altogether. Rising, Adam picks his way across sleeping bodies to the door.

Outside first light is visible, the high cloud that covers the sky pearl-grey and pink, its beauty at odds with the fury just gone. The wind has dropped as well, but as he steps away from the church the evidence of its passage is everywhere. On all sides trees lie tumbled and bent, branches and leaves spread across the open ground. Further down, great pools of water cover the road and footpath.

There is something extraordinary about the scale of the destruction, and as he reaches the end of the path he stops, struck by the silence, the sense of stillness.

'I didn't hear you get up,' Summer says behind him.

He turns. 'I didn't want to wake you.'

'Did you sleep?'

'Not really. Is Noah awake?'

'Not yet.'

Behind them the vicar and a couple of others have appeared.

'I think we need to get out of here,' Summer says.

'Why?'

'It's hard to tell because everything's so confused, but there's stuff on the feeds saying the embankments have given way. And even if they haven't there's a lot of water upstream that will be heading down. Fast. We need to get to higher ground.'

'Or find somewhere we can shelter. But either way we need to move quickly.'

Out on the road the water is already rising, spilling over the gutters and footpaths and filling ditches. Although it is not moving fast it makes walking difficult, and once again Adam finds himself carrying Noah.

With so much water there are few cars around, and those that are do not stop for them. Before they left the church they had debated trying to steal one, but neither knew how, and both feared the time they might waste searching houses for keys.

Because the networks are only intermittently operational, most of what they know is chatter, a jumble of images and warnings, but several things are clear. First, the embankments have indeed given way, collapsing before the combined pressure of a king tide and the storm surge, and the water is pouring in. London is flooded as well, as is much of the country to the west and north.

Occasionally they pass others on the road; sometimes they wave, or exchange information, but most often they simply bend their heads and hurry on. Now and again they hear shouting, the breaking of glass. Twice there is the sound of gunshots.

More than once they see people loading electrical goods into cars and vans. After an hour or so they come around a corner to find a supermarket, set slightly below the level of the road behind a partly flooded car park. The sliding doors are jammed open and through them figures can be seen moving around inside, while out the front half a dozen men and women are stashing things into cars. Passing Noah to Summer, Adam tells her to wait for him.

The floor is submerged under several centimetres

of water. By the checkouts a young man with short dreadlocks and a girl in a gold tracksuit are busy rifling one of the tills, stuffing cash into their pockets. Adam raises his hands to signal he means them no harm, breathing a sigh of relief when the man tilts his head as if to indicate he will not interfere.

Although the shelves have already been stripped, he manages to find several bottles of mineral water and a few blocks of chocolate. Moving quickly he crams them into his bag, together with a torch and a couple of packets of biscuits.

He is almost done when he hears a cry from the front of the store. Remembering the couple by the till he turns back as quietly as he can, but before he reaches the end of the aisle he sees the water has become a tide flowing inward.

Swinging his bag over his shoulder he fights his way out the door and across the car park to where Summer and Noah are waiting. Grabbing Noah's hand he points to a building on the other side of the road, and together the three of them begin to wade towards it.

The water is knee-deep now and moving fast, making it difficult to remain upright. Halfway across Summer slips, stumbling sideways; Adam pulls her up and the three of them struggle on.

The building is three storeys high with a turret on one

corner and a short flight of stairs running up to the main door. Scrambling out of the water they bound up the stairs, only to discover the door is locked.

Adam rattles it several times, cursing. Next to him Summer points to a window a little further along. 'There!' she says.

He grabs Noah and descends into the stream while Summer hauls herself up onto the sill. Pulling her sleeve down she smashes the glass with her elbow, and kicks the shards out of the way with the sole of her shoe. As soon as she is done he passes Noah up, then grasps her hand to clamber up himself, but as he reaches the sill she gasps. Turning, he looks back.

At first all that is visible is the rising water, the refuse floating by. But then he hears a rushing noise, accompanied by creaking and grinding like wind. And then, at the street's end, he sees it. It seems so improbable it's difficult to be afraid, for it is as if the water is pouring towards them in a sloping wall, a liquid hill that moves faster than any of them could run, a wave that does not end but comes and comes and comes.

Beside him Noah whimpers, then Summer shouts, 'Run!' and they do, clattering through the flat to the front door. In the lobby they race up the stairs to the first floor, then on to the second, where two doors open off the landing; taking one each Summer and Adam throw themselves against them, beating and shouting. From downstairs they hear breaking glass and what sounds like metal tearing, until all at once the front door gives way and the water floods in, filling the lobby and surging up the stairs. Stepping back Adam slams his shoulder into the door in front of him, first once, then twice, but to no avail. As he steps back for a third attempt he sees Noah kneeling by the mat in front of the other door, a key in his hand.

Inside the flat they check each room, to be sure they are alone. The place is small, sparsely furnished. In the bedroom a cupboard stands open, a half-filled suitcase lies on the bed. Adam is standing next to it when Summer appears in the doorway; he has time to see her notice it and turn away. When he follows her to the living room she has opened the window and is standing looking out, Noah beside her.

Outside the water is still rising, the level now above the ground-floor windows. Cars and bins and refuse are pouring past, borne by the torrent, swirling and colliding as they sweep along the road. In the park across the street the top of a child's swing protrudes, the water breaking around it in a wave: as they watch, the level moves steadily up it until the swing vanishes. Next to him Noah is shivering. Extending a hand he places it on the boy's shoulder and feels him pull away.

Then Summer lets out a small cry, and looking down Adam sees a woman and two children a little way upstream. The woman is struggling as the water swirls her along, one hand clenched around the collar of the younger child, the other grasping frantically for the second as he tumbles just out of reach. As they pass the window she makes one last effort, but the boy is too far away. He is caught behind a car and swept under. Without speaking Adam draws Noah away from the window, guiding him back to the middle of the room.

By midday the water level seems to have peaked, the raging cataract giving way to a swiftly flowing river, its surface creased here and there by boils and rips as it passes over obstacles and declivities beneath. The heat has returned as well, the temperature rising precipitously as the sky clears. In the flat the air is thick, hot and still, fetid with the smell of the water below.

Realising it may be some time before they are able to move on, Summer elects to go and search some of the other flats for food and water, leaving Adam alone with Noah. Perhaps unsurprisingly after the events of the past twenty-four hours, the boy is not interested in speaking to Adam, or in exploring his surroundings; instead he sandwiches himself into a corner between the bed and the wall, and drawing his knees up loses himself in his screen.

As the day wears on Adam is struck again by how vulnerable the boy seems. At first he had thought it was mostly a function of his extreme thinness, the rigidity with which he holds himself, but he sees now it is more than that. Where another child might place the screen on their knees Noah holds it up against his face, mumbling and poking at it as if trying to drown out something he cannot put out of his mind.

Yet affecting as he finds Noah's vulnerability, it is Summer's responses to the boy that are most painful to observe. Tired, stressed, anxious, she cannot seem to stop herself growing impatient with him, or finding fault with his behaviour, reactions she regrets almost immediately.

'Jesus, Noah,' she snaps when he refuses the biscuits and cheese she has found, 'you have to eat.'

It is late afternoon before the boy finally emerges from his corner beside the bed. With so little for him to do, Summer does not seek to prevent him looking through the rooms, sitting on the bed and going through the drawers. She is in the living room with Adam when Noah reappears and asks where the owner of the flat has gone.

Adam and Summer exchange a glance.

'I don't know,' Summer says. 'Perhaps they went to one of the crisis centres.'

'Like the church?'

Summer nods. 'Perhaps.'

'But what about the water?'

'I'm sure they will have had some plan.'

'But that lady, this morning, those kids.'

Adam touches the boy's shoulder. 'Let's not talk about it,' he says quietly.

It is after ten before it finally grows dark. Although Noah shows no signs of tiredness Summer insists he lie down on the bed, but because he is frightened he wants Summer to stay with him, leaving Adam alone.

Through the window the night is still, warm, the only sound that of the water moving by, the only light the moon, the massing girdle of the Milky Way. Some time after eleven Summer reappears. Crossing to where Adam sits, she looks out.

'They're so bright,' she says, indicating the stars.

'With the power down, there are no lights to interfere with them.'

Summer is silent for a moment. 'They make everything down here seem insignificant, don't they?'

'I suppose it is, if you look at it from that perspective.'

She is quiet again. 'I wonder what did happen to the person who lived here.'

'Nothing good.'

'How many do you think are dead?'

'A lot.' Adam looks at her staring out over the water, her face unreadable.

When she finally speaks again her voice is more distant. 'What do you think is going to happen?'

'I don't know. We keep talking about trying to stop what's happening, slow it down somehow, but I'm not sure that's even possible any more. There are so many of us, and resources are stretched so thin the system can't survive unless there's some kind of radical change. The problem is we're so busy stumbling from one disaster to the next we can't get any distance, can't see what's happening for what it is.'

'You mean the end?'

'A point of transition.'

'You were good with him today,' Summer says, more softly.

Adam smiles. 'He's a nice kid.'

'He likes you. Trusts you even.'

'What will you do?'

'After this?'

Adam nods. 'You can't go back. You know that.'

'I'm not alone in that,' she snaps.

He flinches.

'I'm sorry. It's been a long couple of days.' She pauses. 'Can I ask you something?' she says at last. 'Did you ever want to leave? When I was a kid?'

'Of course.'

'I don't mean leave Mum, I mean leave me.'

What he wants to say is that he loves her, that he always did, and that she is still his child. But all he says is, 'Never.'

Summer doesn't reply. She is so alone, he thinks, so lost, and it frightens him, not because of what she might do to others, but what she might do to herself.

The next day dawns hot and humid. The water has begun to recede, exposing the windows of the ground floor again. On their screens and overlays there are reports of thousands drowned, together with images Adam decides Noah does not need to see.

'When will we be able to leave?' the boy asks over a breakfast of crackers and cheese plundered from one of the flats.

'I'm not sure,' Adam says. 'In a day or two.'

'Tomorrow?'

'Perhaps, though probably not.'

'The next day?'

'Maybe,' Adam says.

As the day progresses the water level continues to drop, and as it does they see the first signs of other survivors. First two helicopters pass overhead, moving fast and high; a little later a makeshift raft with half a dozen men and women on it floats by. They look filthy and exhausted, and one lies flat, his leg bound up in a splint, but when Adam calls out to them several wave their hands and call back.

That night he sleeps on the sofa in the living room again. Alone in the dark he turns his overlays on, flicks through the feeds. There are so many reports it is difficult to make sense of them, to get a clear idea of the scale of the disaster, so finally he gives up and logs into his own archives. He finds himself pulling up images from the past, photos of him and Ellie before their separation, of Summer as a child, eventually stumbling upon a series taken when she was three, outside the house he moved to when he and Ellie separated. She is wearing a blue dress and mugging for the camera, her hands raised in imaginary tiger's paws, her face contorted in a devilish roar. Looking at her image suspended in the air above him he has to fight the urge to reach out and try to touch it.

He wakes early, the light from the window filling the room. Outside the moon is still visible, and in the dawn the water's expanse spreads like ruffled silk beneath the colourless sky. Not for the first time he is struck by the beauty of the planet's transformation, the indifferent majesty of the change that is taking place.

It is nearly six when Summer appears. During the night he woke to the sound of an engine in the distance, and in the quiet that followed its passing he heard her awake in the next room: not surprisingly she now looks tired.

'You're up,' she says.

'For a while.'

She comes to stand next to him and he is struck by a sense of something different in her manner.

'Is everything okay?' he asks.

She looks at him briefly, then away. 'Sure,' she says. 'Fine.'

'Is Noah . . .?'

'Sleeping.' She turns to look at the bottles on the table. 'We need to get out, find water and food.'

'If the water drops enough we can try today.'

And so, come late afternoon, they descend the stairs, wade out into the street. The water is waist-deep, but flowing slowly enough not to be a problem. Now it is possible to see the full scale of the destruction: cars and trees banked against buildings and fences, scrap piled upon them, windows damaged or missing, walls standing at all angles. A few hundred metres down the road a car has been rammed through the front wall of a block of flats; a little further on the entire roof of a house rests upside down but intact in a stand of trees by the side of the road.

There are other, grimmer sights as well. More than once they come across bodies caught in the wreckage. A man pinned to a wall by a car, a woman face down in a sump, a girl hanging suspended in the branches of an overturned tree. At first they try to shield Noah's eyes, but after the third body they give up, and just move past them in silence.

Yet not everyone they come upon is dead. As they make

their way along the road they see people in the distance, some working to retrieve things from houses or loading them onto makeshift rafts, others wading through the water, dragging bags and boxes, dogs and cats, bearing children on their shoulders.

The going is not easy: the water is filthy, brown with mud and slick with oil and sewage, the ground beneath it uneven and treacherous. More than once they slip and fall, fighting to keep their faces above the surface as they sprawl forward, to prevent the water entering their mouths and noses.

Finally, as dusk is approaching, they come to a patch of higher ground surmounted by a military tent of some sort. Inside several men and women in uniform can be seen; in front of it two soldiers are supervising a small crowd of people who are filling their bottles at a line of plastic water butts mounted on pallets. Lowering Noah to the ground Adam approaches thirstily, taking one of the proffered bottles and filling it at the tap, passing it to the boy before filling another for himself.

At the next butt Summer is filling her bottle; she catches his eye for a moment. But Noah has seen the soldiers, is asking about their guns and armour, and Adam lets the boy lead him towards the nearest. To his relief the soldier is friendly, smiling at Noah, asking him how old he is. Something in Summer's expression snagging in his mind, Adam glances over his shoulder, but she is gone.

'Is this your son?' the soldier asks.

'Grandson,' he says, touching the boy's shoulder. 'Noah.'

Noah reaches up and takes his hand. Adam grips it tight, no longer sure whether he is holding on for the boy's sake or for his own.

THE
KEEPER
OF BEES

A week after she moves into her new house Ellie locks the door and strikes out towards the hills on the far side of the valley. The day is unseasonably cool, a south-westerly blowing down from the mountains pushing the clouds overhead, but out of the wind the sun is still hot.

Once the land below was farmland, given over to cows and sheep and horses: she remembers driving through here as a child, gazing out at fields and sheds. In the twenties or thirties it was sold off to one of the carbon credit schemes, and partially planted with native trees and genetically engineered plants. When the schemes went bankrupt the planting was abandoned, and the land left to run wild, the only reminders of its former lives the straggly rows of trees and the old farm buildings scattered here and there amongst them.

Her plan was to walk to the top of the hill and then

strike back towards the road, but as she climbs she finds herself veering west, attracted by the view down to the river and the mountains beyond, their flanks the colour of thunderclouds. On this side of the ridge the larger trees give way to stands of stringybark and the occasional yellow box, many covered with the lumpy excrescences of genetically engineered lichen and bloatmoss, their presence jarring.

In the lee of the hill it is warmer, and after a few minutes she unpeels her jacket and ties it around her waist. Making a mental note to bring a bottle of water next time she goes out walking she starts up the hill again, but after a couple of steps she notices a wooden, box-like structure half hidden behind a tree off to her left.

Wondering whether it might be an old weather station, or perhaps some kind of security device, she walks towards it, but halfway there she notices the bees swirling around it.

Suddenly worried she is trespassing she glances around. Reassured that she is alone, she moves forward to stand beside the tree. The hive is old, its white paint chipped and peeling, the grass around its base long. Despite the breeze the bees are active, circling the hive, crawling in and out, the sound of them frowzy and warm. When one buzzes past her face she lifts a hand and ducks, but almost immediately another lands on her sleeve.

This time she doesn't brush it off but instead pauses, struck by the improbable, clumsy way it moves, legs twitching, wings ready to take off again. It is beautiful, not just as a thing in itself but for the small wonder of its presence, its strange mixture of the alien and the familiar. Extending a finger she touches the fabric in front of it, observing the way it pulls back, the flash of aggression before it launches itself into the air, circling past her face so that she must duck once more.

Moving quietly she retreats a short distance, flicks on her overlays to check for tags on this location. Surprised to find there aren't any, she searches references to bees nearby, this time bringing up a few links for shops selling honey, together with a testimonial for the market a few kilometres up the road from her house. But no mention of apiarists or local production.

She finds two more hives on the walk back, both placed in such a way that they are unlikely to be noticed from the valley below. As with the first, they have been there long enough for the grass to grow up around their bases, but not long enough for anybody to have tagged them or attached any information about who owns them or what they're doing there.

It is after lunch by the time she gets back, and she is hot and sweaty and tired. She takes down her teapot and finds herself thinking again of the bee on her sleeve, its awkward movement and stumpy body, as she pours the water, lets the leaves release their fragrance.

The next morning she heads up to the hives again. She is not entirely sure what it is she is looking for, only that there is something about the bees she needs to explore further.

It is almost ten by the time she reaches the first of them and the bees are already active, bumping busily through the surrounding scrub and congregating on the blossom of the yellow box. Several times one swerves past her head, or circles around her and then veers away.

Once she is close enough she puts down her bag, and taking out a jar begins circling the yellow box tree beside her, trying to choose a bee to catch. Eventually she decides on a clump of flowers, and lifting the jar towards it chivvies one of the bees off the blossom and into its mouth. But as she closes the lid she hears movement behind her. Startled, she turns to find a man standing there.

'What are you doing?' he asks.

'Catching a bee,' she says, rising to her full height.

He looks at the jar in her hand and then at her face. He is about her age, black hair turning grey, and while his clothes are cheap and probably second-hand, he holds himself with a confidence that belies them.

'And why are you doing that?'

This time she hears the trace of an accent in his voice. Indian, perhaps Pakistani.

Realising how peculiar the truth will sound – that she wanted the bee to study and photograph – she slips the jar into her bag.

'Are they yours?' she asks. 'The hives, I mean?'

The man considers her for a second or two. 'They are.'

'All of them?'

'Are you from the government?'

Thrown off balance by the question, Ellie laughs. 'No,' she says. 'I'm an artist.'

He seems confused. 'An artist?'

She nods. 'I just moved in nearby, but nobody told me about the hives.'

Although she had meant her words to be reassuring, he looks uncomfortable.

'You aren't going to report them?'

Now it is her turn to be confused. 'Report them? Why would I do that?'

When he doesn't answer she takes a step away. 'I should be going,' she says.

The beekeeper still doesn't reply but neither does he attempt to prevent her leaving. When she looks back he is staring after her, arms by his side, his face not hostile but somehow anxious.

She walks home briskly, fighting the urge to break into a run, but by the time she reaches the house the encounter at the hive has already begun to seem curious rather than unsettling. Extracting the jar from her bag she carries it through to her studio and sets it on the windowsill, then sits down to examine her captive. Where a fly would be still, the bee crawls and bumps about with such persistence she finds herself wondering how it stores enough energy to keep going. About its thorax and head the orange-brown fur is thicker than she had imagined; coupled with the glistening architecture of the wings, its softness lends the tiny creature a curiously archaic quality, somehow blurring the boundaries between insect and mammal.

Turning to her screen she asks it to locate some information about bee physiology, and for a few minutes she listens to it read out excerpts, feeling the ideas coalescing in her mind. It is often like this for her, the shape of a project coming before she has the detail, as if the idea were already present, inchoate; she has learned to trust this feeling, to give the connections time to form.

* * *

The next morning, she packs a bag and retraces her tracks to the hives a second time. When she arrives she is relieved to find the beekeeper absent, and putting down her bag she seats herself on a fallen trunk to watch the bees and listen to their heavy sound. Overnight she has been reading about the cultivation of bees in Egypt and Sumer, and the evidence from rock art and elsewhere of the harvesting of wild honey in Mesolithic times; in the silence of the hillside she finds herself reminded of this history, the idea that humans have shared the world with these creatures for so long filling her with something that is not quite wonder, not quite grief, but somehow both.

She is turning these thoughts over in her mind when she catches sight of the beekeeper heading down the slope towards her. Suddenly struck by the thought that he may have some kind of surveillance nearby, she glances around for a camera, but nothing is visible.

'Hello again,' she says as he reaches the clearing.

He has a backpack slung over one shoulder but otherwise is dressed as before.

'Hello,' he replies, eyeing her carefully as he sets his backpack down.

'I'm sorry about yesterday,' she says. 'I didn't mean —'

'You've not been at other hives?' he asks brusquely.

'No. Why?'

'It's important,' he says, coming closer. 'You're sure?'

'Of course,' she says. 'Why would I lie about it?'

He considers her for a few seconds. Then, quite abruptly, he relaxes. 'Okay,' he says. 'I'm sorry, I don't mean to be rude.'

'Don't worry about it. Although I don't understand why it would matter.'

'ACCD,' he says.

'I'm sorry?'

He looks at her sharply. 'Accelerated colony collapse disorder. Bee colonies dying.'

'I thought the collapses slowed down back in the twenties, after they banned the insecticides that were causing them?'

'They did. But in the past couple of years they've started again, worse than ever. People have been trying to quarantine the hives, but it doesn't seem to work.'

He seems to be scrutinising her. When he finally speaks again his voice is gentler, less confrontational. 'The other day you said you are an artist.'

'That's right.'

'And why are you interested in my bees?'

'I'm not exactly sure yet. I have an idea for a project involving them, but I'm still thinking it through.'

Again he seems to consider his next move. 'Please,' he says after a few seconds. 'Watch this.'

Opening his bag he takes out heavy gloves and a hat with a gauze veil and puts them on, adjusting the gloves so they seal about his sleeves. Once he is done he lights a small device, pumping the handle so smoke emerges. Then, pulling down his veil, he advances on the hive and removes the top. The bees rise, swirling around him, their buzzing louder, more agitated. Setting the lid down he picks up the smoker, scattering the bees with the coils of grey smoke.

Inside the hive are a line of frames; drawing out the first he turns it on its side, revealing the golden comb, a few bees still moving on it. Setting the frame upon a tray he clears the last of the bees with the smoker, then takes a metal scraper and slides it down the face of the frame. Viscous honey oozes lumpily into the tray.

Replacing the frame, he draws out the next and repeats the process, and then again, until the hive has been cleared. Then he locks the lid in place and makes his way back to Ellie, bees still swirling around him.

She waits until he removes his mask to approach him.

'Do they ever sting you?'

'Of course,' he says, folding his mask away. 'But not often. I think they know me.'

Perhaps she looks sceptical because he smiles. 'You think that is ridiculous?'

She shrugs. 'Maybe.'

'They know things, bees. They become used to you. The hives live and last. It is not so unreasonable to think they might have memories.' He smiles once more. 'But they still sting me sometimes.'

'I've never seen honey harvested before,' Ellie says.

'No?' He uncovers the tray and takes a spoon from his bag. 'Here,' he says.

She takes the spoon carefully, cupping her other hand beneath it. The honey is thick and gold, so dark it is almost brown, with lumps of wax and comb still visible here and there. Closing her mouth around the spoon she finds the taste so sweet and rich and impossibly deep that without thinking she closes her eyes. When she opens them he is watching her.

'It is good?'

'It's amazing. Is it always like this?'

'Sometimes. It depends on the season, on which flowers are nearby.'

She nods, the spiced sweetness of the honey still burning in her nostrils. There is something fascinating about the idea of a substance that changes with the seasons in this way, a reminder of a time when the planet still moved to its own cycles.

Taking the tray he begins to transfer the honey into a plastic container. When he is done he slips it into his backpack and stands up. 'Perhaps you can tell me something of this project you are thinking about?'

As they make their way down the ridge she tells him the little she has mapped out already. That she would like to take photos of the bees and the interior of the hives in close-up, and possibly build models of them both; that she has an image of bees alive and moving as well. He listens quietly and attentively, only interrupting when they reach the road.

'This would be online?' he asks. 'Or in a gallery somewhere?'

She hesitates. 'Virtual, I think.'

'Perhaps we should talk about it some more later. My name is Amir.'

'Ellie,' she says, and pings her number to him. 'And yes, I'd like that.'

* * *

Back home she checks her messages, several of which are from Adam regarding Noah, whom she is minding later in the week, an arrangement she is, as usual, simultaneously looking forward to and apprehensive about.

When she first learned of the boy's existence twelve months before, she had felt physically ill, the fact of Summer's decision to conceal Noah from them throwing her completely off balance for weeks.

It didn't help that the world seemed to be falling apart as well, the floods in England followed by deluges in northern Europe and Burma, the escalation of the war in the Middle East and the horrors in Chicago. In the weeks following Adam's call from London, and the struggle to get Noah evacuated to Australia, she lurched uncontrollably between anger and regret for her failures as a parent.

As the months passed she regained a degree of equilibrium. She can still become angry if she thinks about it, but her initial sense of betrayal has lessened, displaced by the reality of the present and, increasingly, a deeper grief about Summer. It never fails to surprise her how easily and irrevocably the present replaces the past, how what had seemed immovable, permanent, simply fades and vanishes.

This change in her feelings also applies to Noah himself. Before she met him she was apprehensive, alarmed by Adam's description of his disorder, and this clouded her early encounters with him, keeping her hyper-alert to unusual or unpredictable behaviour. But while there is no question the boy can be difficult, that his refusal to sleep at regular hours and his sudden, unpredictable bouts of anxiety and agitation are unnerving and exhausting, he also has an intelligence and gentleness she has come to love.

Because this visit is his first to her new home, the plan is for Adam to stay for the afternoon, only leaving once Noah feels comfortable. It is an arrangement that was reached after some negotiation between Adam and her – a process, she thinks ruefully, they might have done well to master sooner.

The appointed day dawns wet, cloud from a cyclone in the north bringing torrential rain, meaning Adam is an hour late when he pulls into the driveway. Ellie watches him lean across to open the door for Noah before leaping out himself, an umbrella over his head, and running to the passenger door. But Noah doesn't move, just sits staring forward, hands clutching the seat. Holding the umbrella higher, Adam crouches to say something, his words inaudible over the rain, and Noah shakes his head.

Glancing up, Adam points towards Ellie and the boy turns to look at her. She waves in welcome, struck by the way his face has changed in the fortnight since she saw him last, the sudden glimpse of the adult he will become.

Finally Noah consents to get out of the car, and huddled together under the umbrella the two of them cross the yard slowly, Adam trying in vain to hurry the boy up.

'Hi, Noah,' she says once they are inside, kneeling down beside him and holding out a hand. Once, he would have shied away from her but now he places his hand in hers, lets her kiss his cheek.

'It's raining,' he says. 'That means we can't use the telescope.'

'It does, although perhaps we'll be able to use it tomorrow.'

'Is it set up?' he asks.

'Out the back,' she says, pointing the way, but Noah is already moving past her.

'What was that all about?' she asks once she and Adam are alone.

He shakes his head. 'I told him he couldn't use his lenses in the car.'

'Ah.' Looking out at the rain, she says, 'Have you got bags?'

Adam looks out with her and smiles. 'I think I might wait.'

In the kitchen she makes tea while Adam brushes water off his shoulders.

'How's he been?' she asks as she hands him his cup.

'Good, I think. School seems to be going better. And he's been excited about coming here.'

'And you?'

'I'm good as well. Busy.'

An awkwardness descends, the mention of Adam's work, of their separate lives, reminding them of a past neither is quite ready to discuss.

'What are you working on?' he asks.

She is about to try to explain her interest in the bees, tell him about finding the hives, when she sees she has a voice call. Excusing herself to Adam she picks up her earpiece.

'Hello,' says an accented voice, 'is this Ellie? This is Amir.'

She surprises herself by smiling. 'Yes, Amir.'

'I'm not interrupting, am I?'

'No, no, not at all. I'm glad you called,' she says. Giving Adam an apologetic glance she stands up and steps into the next room.

'You talked about an exhibition. I thought perhaps I would like to know more.'

'Yes,' she says, 'of course. I can't talk now, but perhaps we could meet. Is there a time that would suit you?'

'Maybe the day after tomorrow?'

'Could you come here?'

'If you would like that.'

Through the door she can see Adam staring out the window.

'Let me send you my address,' she says.

The next two days pass slowly. Although she has had Noah before, it is always a shock to be reminded of the effort involved in minding a child full-time, especially one like Noah. While Adam has hired a carer to help him with the boy, when he stays with her they are alone together, meaning she is hostage to his wakefulness in the evenings and his relentless focus on particular activities.

She has grown better at accommodating him, but it is not always easy, and on the second night she loses her temper with him several times, frustrated with his constant circling through the kitchen and the living room and back again, his obsessive questions about when the weather will clear. As always at such moments she regrets her irritation almost immediately. And she is also reminded of what it must have been like for Summer, alone with him all that time.

On the morning of the day Amir is due to visit she rises

early to find Noah already up, his lenses on, absorbed in exploring one of the virtual worlds he spends hours in every day. Deciding there is no need to disturb him she makes his breakfast, assembling the food the only way he will eat it – white toast with the crusts removed and a boiled egg – and setting it down in front of him she heads out to her studio to begin organising her materials in preparation for Amir's visit.

Although she has had little time to think about it over the past couple of days, Ellie has become convinced the project will be substantial, that the bees and their presence contain some implication she can work with. Knowing Noah will be content in his virch for as long as he is left undisturbed, she begins mapping new ideas, only looking up when her system reminds her it is almost ten and Amir is due in fifteen minutes.

Suddenly aware that she hasn't heard from Noah since she put his breakfast in front of him she goes back through to the kitchen, the living room, but both are empty. Anxiously she calls his name, once, and then again, louder, moving quickly through the rooms until finally she comes to the front of the house and sees that the door is ajar.

Racing out into the bright air she shouts his name, but there is no answer. Her legs trembling, she runs to the gate, stands staring up and down the road; still there is no sign of him. Activating her earpiece, she calls up Noah's number but it is offline. She calls Adam, heart pounding. He answers cheerfully but she cuts him off immediately.

'Noah's disappeared.'

'What do you mean?'

'He's vanished. I was in my studio and when I came out he'd gone.'

There is a moment of silence. When Adam speaks again his voice is deliberately calm. 'Okay,' he says, 'he won't have gone far. Have you tried calling him?'

'Of course I did. He's offline.'

'That doesn't mean much, the network isn't great out there.'

'Do you have any idea where he might be?'

'He was talking about looking for somewhere to set up the telescope the other day. Perhaps he's gone to do that.'

Ellie is already heading down the road. 'Did he say where?'

'No, but I guess he'd be looking for a patch of clear ground away from the road.'

As he speaks Ellie receives an alert, and remembers her arrangement with Amir. 'I've got to go,' she says. 'I've got somebody coming, I need to tell them to cancel.'

She calls up Amir's number; he answers almost at once.

'I'm sorry,' she says, trying to keep the note of panic out of her voice, 'I'm not going to be able to make it this morning. My grandson has disappeared.'

'Disappeared?'

'Yes. I left him in the kitchen and when I came back he was gone.'

'Could somebody have come in and taken him?'

'I don't think so. I think he's just wandered off.'

'Are his parents nearby?'

'No,' she says. 'His grandfather is in the city.'

'Where are you? I will come help you look.'

'Yes,' she says, 'please.'

At Amir's suggestion she heads back up the road while he checks the old farm buildings. As she moves further from the house she runs faster, calls louder, fear like a space inside her. About five hundred metres from the house she notices a track leading into the scrub and heads up it, still calling for him over and over. Away from the road it is quieter, the trees closing in, the silence triggering memories of stories about children getting lost in the bush, or being kidnapped, their bodies turning up months or years later in some out-of-the-way place.

And then, just as she is slowing, ready to head back to the road, she gets a call from Amir.

'Amir?' she asks breathlessly, but before she can finish he is speaking over her, telling her not to worry, he has him.

She slumps against a tree, her legs trembling.

'Ellie?'

'Is he okay?'

'He is all right. He was sitting in one of the houses down here. Do you want to talk to him?'

'Yes,' she says, and a moment later Noah joins the call.

'Noah,' she says, 'where *were* you?'

'I was looking for somewhere to put the telescope,' he says.

'You can't just walk off like that, without telling me where you're going.'

Noah pauses. 'All right.'

'Are you okay?'

'Yes,' he says petulantly.

Ellie ignores his tone. 'Can you go with Amir? He's a friend.'

There is no response.

'Noah?'

'Okay,' he says at last, his voice sullen.

By the time she nears the house, the two of them are

visible on the road ahead. Seeing her approach, Amir points her out to Noah but the boy hangs back, his face turned away as if afraid, or ashamed.

Kneeling down she looks up at him. 'I'm not angry,' she says. 'But you frightened me really badly. I didn't know where you were.'

'Sorry,' Noah says, his face still turned away.

'It's okay,' she says. 'Will you walk with me now?'

Back in the house she shuffles Noah into the living room and agrees he can play his game for a while. Watching him pick up his lenses she feels her anxiety of a few minutes before replaced by a sudden wash of love, made raw by fear for his vulnerability, the difficulties that lie ahead for him.

Turning back to Amir, who is standing in the doorway, she asks, 'Would you like something to eat? A drink?'

Amir smiles. 'Some water will be fine.'

Ellie opens the fridge, takes out one of the bottles. Since the water restrictions tightened she has taken to bottling water when it is available and storing it. Placing two glasses on the table she sits down opposite him.

'Thank you again for helping find him,' she says. 'It was very kind of you.'

Amir smiles. 'Please, it was nothing.'

'It wasn't, and I appreciate it.'

In the living room Noah makes a sound that might be pleasure and might be irritation. Amir catches Ellie's eye.

'He is your grandson?'

'My daughter's son.'

Perhaps hearing the hesitation in her words, Amir does not press the point. 'You have him a lot?'

'No. He lived in England until recently.'

'It is not easy, I think, minding children who are not your own.'

Grateful for his reluctance to press her Ellie smiles. 'I'm sure you have better things to do than sit here. Perhaps I can show you some of what I'm proposing?'

'Thank you,' Amir says. 'I would like that.'

Ellie often finds the process of discussing her projects before they are fully realised uncomfortable, embarrassing even, but as she outlines her ideas to Amir she is encouraged by his tact and thoughtfulness, the care with which he listens and examines the images and plans she has assembled. Even his questions are intelligent, revealing a genuine interest in the thinking behind the things she shows him.

'It is very impressive,' Amir says when she is done.

'Thank you,' Ellie replies. 'You can see why it matters to me that I work with real bees, though?'

'I do,' Amir says.

'But?'

He looks uncomfortable. 'It is not as simple as you think. I am frightened for the bees.'

'Because of the colony collapses?'

He nods, and she glimpses some deeper reticence in him, a sadness, perhaps, of which the bees are only one part.

'Is it that bad?'

'I am afraid it might be. None of the collapses before have been anything like this. It began in Europe but spread through America and Asia in less than a year. For a while we were protected, but now the colonies here are dying as well.'

'What's causing it?'

'Nobody knows. Some people believe it's due to toxicity, chemicals in the environment. Others say it's about climate. Some think it's viral, or a combination of all three.'

'And you?'

'I don't know. Some species seem to be more resistant, especially the native bees. But last summer the native colonies started collapsing as well.'

She draws a breath. His face is careful, closed, as if afraid of what he might say next. When she speaks her voice is quieter, more careful.

'Were you always a beekeeper?'

He looks at her incredulously. 'What, you think I kept bees back in Bangladesh?'

'I don't know. You seem to know a lot about them.'

'I was a doctor,' he says. 'In Dhaka.'

'Really?'

'That surprises you?'

Ellie grins. 'A little, I suppose. How did you end up here?' she asks, then catches herself. 'If you don't mind me asking, that is.'

She sees his reticence again, knows it for the wound it is.

'After the government fell, we fled.'

'We?'

'I had a wife and a daughter.'

'What happened?'

'They died,' he says quietly.

Ellie watches him without speaking. 'And then you came here?' she asks at last.

He nods. 'I was in the camps for a long time. One day I escaped. I didn't know where to go. I was hurt in my heart, depressed, almost catatonic, but I couldn't bear the thought of them taking me back there so I hitchhiked my way south.'

'And the bees?'

'They came later. After I came south I met a man who

said he'd been working on a property out west. He gave me the name of somebody there who might help me. But on the way I met another man, an Iraqi. He was sick and needed somebody to take the hives.'

Amir is silent then. Ellie wants to take his hand but is worried he might not welcome her touch.

'It is foolish, I know, but the bees helped me. The first time they landed on me, enveloped me, it was as if I was no longer simply me but part of them, as if they connected me to something that went beyond myself.' Amir's eyes meet hers. 'Perhaps you think I am being ridiculous?'

Ellie shakes her head. 'No,' she says. 'Not at all.'

That night Noah agrees to go to bed earlier than normal, disappearing into his room almost without resistance. Relieved to find herself alone Ellie retreats to her studio and calls up her research.

Unsettled by her conversation with Amir she begins by seeking out more material about ACCD, and the more she reads, the better she understands his concern. This new wave of collapses is certainly different from those in the past, both in severity and distribution. In some parts of Europe and the United States bee populations have gone altogether, and farmers have been importing bees to pollinate their crops.

Yet it is not the speed with which colonies are collapsing that is most frightening, but the fact that there appears to be no pattern to the process, no single factor that can be isolated as a cause. In some places the problem seems related to the release of genetically engineered plants into the wild, but elsewhere it seems to be about infections overwhelming already stressed colonies, or the build-up of pesticides or other toxins. The collapses are either due to a convergence of factors or, perhaps more alarmingly, some kind of spontaneous event.

She remembers Adam suggesting many years before that something like this might happen, that the planet's ecosystems could reach a point where they simply began to collapse, seemingly spontaneously, the addition of one more factor to the equation triggering a phase of transition, in much the way that a single snowflake can be said to cause an avalanche. It was a process he claimed was visible in the die-offs of frogs and birds, the disappearance of marine species, as well as in the increasingly convulsive changes in the climate, the accelerating feedback loops of melting ice and methane release. And in time, according to Adam, something would trigger a similar collapse in the human population, causing it to crash as well.

As she reads it is not just the bees she is thinking of, but Amir. He is illegal, that is clear, yet so much else about him is mysterious. Where does he live? Why has he chosen to help her? Her younger self might have just accepted these gaps in her knowledge of him, but at her age it is difficult not to be wary. Briefly she considers calling Bec, asking her opinion, but already able to hear her friend's incredulity, she decides not to. And so instead she finds herself reading about the illegals, trying to imagine their lives. Their presence is a debate that has filled the media for as long as she can remember, a constant rumble of anger and paranoia, but over the years she has learned to tune it out. Tonight she finds herself assailed by it all over again, by the descriptions of the camps, the random harassment by police, the detention and forced expulsion of anyone the government deems undesirable. It is ridiculous, monstrous. Where, after all, are those who have sought refuge here meant to go? The islands of the Pacific are disappearing, Bangladesh is gone, as is much of Burma and coastal India; hundreds of millions have been displaced and are in need of assistance. Yet in the face of their suffering, politicians do little more than posture and parrot slogans.

Eventually, vertiginous with agitation and despair, she

puts down her screen and steps out into the night. In his room Noah is asleep, his soft snores audible through the open window. Somewhere to the west lightning dances against the purple sky; overhead a flying fox crashes and shrieks amongst the branches. Turning back towards the house she looks in through her studio window, sees the insects moving like a halo in the light, silent but for the beat of the moths against the flyscreens. She had thought that getting older would mean it got easier, that she might feel more settled. Yet standing here now she feels as raw as a teenager, her confusion like an ache within her.

In the weeks that follow she begins work in earnest. As with most of her projects the installation will be accessible through lenses and overlays, which means that much can be done by fabricators, software agents capable of constructing the virtual environment that will house the installation. But as is her habit she spends considerable time thinking through the arrangement of the spaces, developing different ways for visitors to interact with her creations.

Although she has already decided that the centrepiece will be a series of virtual sculptures and two-metre close-up photos of the bees, she knows these will need to be complemented by video sequences, some constructed by her from footage of Amir's hives, others sourced from archives. Finding material suitable for these latter elements is a slow process, a matter of hunting through reams of information online, although in fact it soon becomes apparent that the pieces which will work best are mostly older – early- and mid-twentieth-century videos transferred from ageing 8mm and 16mm film, their images flickering by slightly too fast. Choosing from amongst them is partly a matter of eliminating those lacking the quality of mute strangeness and unrecoverability she requires, but while the possibilities are many and various, encompassing old footage of bees moving through hives, bees on flowers, bees crawling over honeycomb or swarming in trees, there is one she cannot put out of her mind. It was shot nearly a century earlier, and shows a man dressed in shirt and pants standing in an orchard with bees swarming onto him, covering first his arms and then rising slowly up as their numbers swelled to obscure his chest, and finally his face and head.

At first she thinks it must be a fake, an early exercise in special effects – certainly it is reminiscent of one of the nitrate dreamscapes of Cocteau or Buñuel – but as she sets it running in an endless loop, the bees massing on his body and face and disappearing over and over and over again, she begins to accept that it is real, not just the bees, but the way in which the man raises his head as they alight on him, his only concession to their presence his closed eyes and mouth, the beatific expression on his face as it vanishes beneath their bodies.

With the videos selected and sequenced, she turns to the other elements of the installation, allowing the project to absorb her, working long into the night. It is always striking to her how often these periods of creativity seem to be connected to the advent of spring, the strange timelessness of the warm evenings, although whether this is innate, a tic in the chemistry of her brain, or a habit ingrained during her time as a student, those formative years when the most intense periods inevitably coincided with the sudden explosion of spring, is unclear to her.

When she lived in the city she would often spend the evenings sitting on the front steps and staring into the night, listening to the sound of the traffic and thrilling to the sense of a secret world unfolding in the sleeping streets. Out here the night is quieter, the sounds – those of shrieking possums and feral cats or the distant barking of dogs – are stranger, less easy, yet the sensation that time is expanding, that a different way of being lies just beneath the skin of the moment, is no less strong.

Occasionally her afternoons or evenings are interrupted by visits from Amir. Despite the gulf between them she quickly finds herself looking forward to his company.

She knows the risks, the possibility of looking foolish, or worse. Every day there are stories about illegals breaking into houses, about muggings and attacks, and while she is certain Amir is not violent, that his interest in her is genuine, she remains uncomfortable with how little she knows about him. Sometimes when she calls him he speaks in a hushed voice, as if he is not alone, not able to speak properly; at other times he is somewhere noisy. Never does he attempt to explain where he is or who he is with.

And then one afternoon he calls and asks if she is alone.

'Why?' she asks. 'Is something wrong?'

'If I give you an address can you come to it?' he asks.

She hesitates. 'Of course,' she says. 'Where are you?'

He gives her directions to a place on the outskirts of the city, half an hour's drive away. The area is unfamiliar – a maze of apartments and houses built around the turn of the century – but eventually she arrives at a block of flats. As she pulls up, Amir appears.

'Thank you for coming,' he says as she climbs out of the car.

'That's fine,' she says. 'What is it?'

He glances up the street as if concerned they are being observed. 'Come inside.'

She follows him up a flight of stairs and into a passageway. At the end of it he stops in front of a door.

'You don't have to agree to any of this,' he says.

Ellie laughs a little uncomfortably. 'I still don't know why I'm here.'

'My friends are inside with their daughter. She is sick, and we need medicine.'

'Why not take her to a hospital?'

Amir hesitates, and as he does Ellie understands. 'You're afraid of being arrested.'

He nods.

'What can I do?' she asks.

The plan is simple. Ellie will drive the girl, Nisha, to a nearby clinic and register her there herself. Because Nisha is a minor Amir thinks that if Ellie says she is her niece from overseas she will be able to use her own ID to have the girl admitted. 'They'll ask you to pay her costs up front because she's not a legal resident,' he says, 'but if you can do that there probably won't be too many difficult questions.'

'And what if there's a problem?'

Amir's jaw tightens. 'There won't be,' he says.

In the car on the way to the clinic Ellie cannot help but

glance at Nisha and her parents, Mishkat and Riya, in the back seat. The girl is ten, small for her age, and dressed in a cheap tracksuit top and an old pair of leggings; sprawled across the seat with her head in her mother's lap she looks very sick indeed, her skin grey.

At the clinic Amir gets out as well.

'I thought you said you couldn't come in?' she says.

'Her parents can't. I'll tell them I'm your friend.'

Ellie wonders if she should object, but before she can say anything Mishkat steps forward and hands Nisha to Amir.

'Please,' Riya says, 'look after her.'

Ellie smiles as confidently as she can, and she and Amir hurry through the doors.

The doctor they are assigned is brief and to the point, his expression barely faltering when Ellie explains Nisha is a niece. 'It's appendicitis,' he says. 'We'll have to operate immediately.'

Ellie looks at Amir, who inclines his head almost imperceptibly.

'Okay,' Ellie tells the doctor. 'If you think it's the only option.'

While Nisha is prepped for surgery Ellie and Amir sit in the waiting room. Outside it is growing dark, the sky through the high window a vivid scarlet and orange.

'You knew it was appendicitis?' Ellie asks, and Amir nods.

'How long did you wait before calling me?'

He does not answer at once. 'Longer than we should have.'

'How long have you known Mishkat and Riya?'

'A year or two. They were in one of the camps out west before that.'

'And you help them with what? Medical advice?'

'I do what I can.'

'How many people do you help?'

He shrugs. 'A few.'

Ellie sits staring at him. 'Why didn't you tell me?' she asks at last.

'Tell you what?'

'About this. About the doctoring. About what you do. I could have helped.'

'Could you? How? We don't just need access to hospitals, we need medicine, schools, jobs, not to be frightened all the time. To be able to buy food without being terrified somebody will become suspicious because we're using cash, or report us to the police because they don't recognise us.'

Shocked by his vehemence Ellie falls silent.

'I'm sorry,' Amir says.

'No, don't be. You have every right to be angry.'

'But not at you.'

The next hour passes slowly, but eventually a nurse appears and beckons them over.

'Nisha's fine,' she says. 'She came through like a trouper.'

Opposite her Amir breaks into a grin.

'When can we see her?' Ellie asks.

The nurse glances at her overlays. 'She's in recovery now, but as soon as she's out we'll let you know.'

'And other visitors?'

'Tomorrow,' the nurse says.

It is growing dark by the time Ellie and Amir emerge. Mishkat and Riya race towards them. 'How is she?' Mishkat asks.

'Okay,' Amir says. 'Resting.'

At Amir's words Mishkat puts his arm around Riya and draws her against him.

'And when can we see her?' asks Riya.

'Not till tomorrow.'

Ellie drives the four of them back in silence. Outside the flat she gets out with Mishkat and Riya. Standing by the car Mishkat bows his head to her.

'Thank you,' he says. Next to him Riya presses her

hands together, tears in the corner of her eyes.

'Please,' Ellie says, 'don't. I only wish I could do more.'

As Mishkat and Riya turn away she looks at Amir. 'You're staying?'

'For a while,' he says.

'You'll let me know if I can help again?'

He smiles. 'I will. And Ellie?'

'Yes?'

'Thank you.'

Although she expects to hear from him the next day, or the day after that, she does not, the time passing quietly in work and walking. More than once she considers calling, asking for news on how Nisha is faring, but she restrains herself, unsure whether she is wary of intruding or wary because she senses that things have changed between the two of them.

On the third day she calls Bec, and for the first time tells her about him, careful to avoid mention of the trip to the hospital.

'He's illegal?' Bec asks disbelievingly.

Ellie tells her he is.

'Oh Jesus, Ellie. You know you can be charged for assisting him?'

'I don't need a lecture,' Ellie says, wondering as she does whether she has made a mistake.

Back in her studio she opens her overlays, calls up some of her notes. She has seen fossils of bees, bodies in stone dating back 140 million years, evidence that they existed alongside the dinosaurs, that they were moving between ancient flowers in the forests of the Cretaceous. It is a dizzying thought, the idea that they have existed for so long, their colonies shifting and changing and evolving as the world altered around them, and one she finds herself returning to. Do individual bees have any conception of time, or is their existence simpler than that, their brief lives lived in the busy rush of the moment? What do they understand of the past, of the future, of the deep well of their history? Do the hives remember? And if they do, what do they make of the collapses, of passing away and out of time?

She is in the kitchen the next day when Bec pings her. 'Have you seen what's happening?' she asks.

'No,' Ellie replies, pulling up her feeds. At first she cannot grasp what she is seeing, what the reports of police and security raiding buildings mean, and she spends several seconds scrolling through video and photos, trying to make sense of the shouting and jolting perspectives before she feels the chill of comprehension.

She pings Amir, and when there is no reply, live-calls him, but still he doesn't answer. Standing up she circles the table, scanning the feeds for more information, before calling him again. Finally she calls Bec back.

'What do you know about what's going on?' she asks.

'Not much. Just that they've been raiding places all over the city. Where's Amir?'

'I don't know. I can't get hold of him.'

'Don't panic,' Bec says. 'It could be nothing. Is there somewhere he might go?'

Ellie thinks of the hives. 'Perhaps. I'm not sure.'

'Do you know where he lives?'

'No.'

She can hear Bec's silent calculation of the meaning behind that ignorance.

'If he has been arrested, where would they take him?'

'I don't know,' Bec says. 'One of the police stations? A processing centre?'

'If I call the police will they tell me whether they've got him?'

'Maybe. I don't know. Do you have a lawyer?'

'No. Would it make a difference?'

'It could. I'll send you the details of my friend Rachel. She might be able to help.'

Ellie pauses. 'Thank you.'

'No worries,' Bec says. 'And Ellie?'

'What?'

'Good luck.'

She calls up the public interface for the security companies who manage the centres, but as she expected they yield nothing. Placing a request with Rachel results in a frustrating conversation with an automated system that takes her details and suggests various courses of action without charge. Then, as she is about to give up, she receives a voice call.

'Ellie?' the caller asks.

'Yes. Is that Rachel?'

'Bec says you've got a friend who's been picked up?' She has the slightly clipped voice of a woman used to dealing with authority from the wrong side of the table.

'That's what I'm trying to find out.'

'Where would he have been?'

'I'm not sure. Somewhere outside the city.'

'Okay. If they've got him he's most likely to be in the

processing centre at Penrith.'

'Is there some way of contacting them, finding out if he's there?'

'They don't release information to the public unless they're next of kin.'

'Perhaps I could go there, ask them in person.'

'They won't tell you even if he is,' Rachel says.

Ellie lifts her hand to her face, pinches her brow. 'Are you sure?'

'Positive,' Rachel says. 'They're not required to release any information. But if you leave it with me I'll see what I can do.'

Once Rachel hangs up Ellie scans the newest reports about the crackdown, searching videos for Amir's face. It now seems that the operation is being coordinated across the entire east coast, with thousands already detained. She understands enough about the laws surrounding illegals to know that if Amir has been caught he is extremely unlikely to be released again, especially given he has already escaped custody once, which means that he will be processed and deported, back to what remains of Bangladesh. The idea is insupportable, unbearable.

Not knowing what else to do, she gets in her car and drives to Mishkat and Riya's, scanning the faces of passers-by as she goes. Around their building there are signs of raids and resistance, groups of people standing in doorways or moving uncertainly through the streets; windows have been broken, cars overturned. Stopping outside Mishkat and Riya's she runs to the door, but as she opens it a woman in a black security uniform appears, her face obscured behind a helmet and visor.

'Sorry,' the woman says. 'This area is restricted.'

'What do you mean, restricted?' Ellie demands.

'I'm afraid we can't divulge details of operational matters,' the woman says. 'Perhaps if you could tell me what business you've got here?'

From somewhere upstairs there is a crash, then shouting.

Ellie takes a step forward but the woman blocks her with her body, the physical threat unmistakeable.

'Perhaps you could give me some ID?' she says. 'It might be useful for us to know why you're here.'

Ellie moves back, suddenly aware she is shaking. 'It doesn't matter,' she says, hating herself as she speaks the words. 'I'll come back later.'

Driving home she has to fight to keep her anger and shame at bay, the argument she should have made circling in her head, her fury only increased by her impotence. How can things have reached the point where people just disappear, where there is no process or review, or recognition they were even here? How can it be that she is so weak she cannot help? How can they have surrendered so much to their worst natures?

By the time she reaches the house her fury has leached away, leaving only emptiness. To the west the sun is already dropping behind the hills; inside she turns on the lights, walks through the empty rooms to her studio. Opening her screen she sees a message saying the first roughs of the sculptures and images for the installation have arrived; pulling them up she turns the sculptures under her hands, marvelling at them. They are beautiful, the chitinous shell of the eyes smooth beneath the yellow of the fur, the glistening transparency of the wings. Yet it is the one in flight she finds herself returning to, amazed by the way in which the legs fold under the body, so that a clumsy shape becomes something impossibly elegant.

With a stab of sadness she realises she was right about the project's strength. Once rendered many thousands of times their own size, the insects are transformed, made wondrous and strange. Likewise the close-ups of their faces – the blankness their eyes reveal when expanded both invite and repel identification; their unknowability is like a space into which one can fall, a reminder of the presence of otherness in the world, and of the loss of its passing.

By the time she has finished examining the roughs it is dark, the sound of crickets rising outside. She should eat but she is not hungry. It is quite possible she will never hear from him again. The mistake is hers, of course, to allow herself to become attached to a man whose life is so parlous, who might disappear at any moment.

Turning the overlays off and removing her lenses she returns to the kitchen, boils water for tea. But as she is warming the pot she hears footsteps outside. For a second or two she stands frozen in place, then, heart thumping in her chest, she races for the door.

In the light from the hall he looks tired and rumpled, but unharmed.

'You're all right,' she says, the words coming in a rush.

He nods.

'I thought . . .'

'I know,' he says. 'I'm sorry.'

'What happened?'

'I was out checking the hives. And while I was there I saw the news about the arrests. I didn't know what to do so I hid.'

'Why didn't you answer my calls?'

'I was scared,' he says.

Ellie realises she is crying. 'I was so frightened.' Reaching out she clasps his hand in hers. 'And the hives?'

'They are okay. At least for now.'

Unslinging his rucksack he draws out a small package. 'Here,' he says, holding it out to her.

She takes it, and unpeeling the paper sees a piece of honeycomb.

'It's for you,' he says. Raising it to her lips she closes her eyes and bites into it, the rush of sweetness filling her mouth. And when she opens her eyes Amir is still there, waiting for her.

A

JOURNAL

OF THE

PLAGUE

YEAR

SEPTEMBER 25

I'm not really sure how to begin this so I'll just begin. My name is Li Lijuan, and today is my sixteenth birthday. I suppose sixteen doesn't seem all that old to a lot of people but it seems old to me, and it got me to thinking about how much I'll actually remember when I'm old. I'll have my lifelogs, obviously, and videos of the things I did and people I knew, but will I have anything to remind me what I thought or felt, or who I was? Because when I look at the vids of when I was eight or ten or even fourteen, all of that has already slipped away, and the only things left are pictures of people and places, half of which I don't even recognise, and all the tags in the world won't remind me of what I was like.

So I've decided I'm going to keep a diary and write down what happens. The idea is it will be for me, so if I want to look at it next year or in a decade or when I'm a hundred, I'll know what my life was like, what I was like. But since even if it is for me some intrepid archaeologist might recover it in a thousand years and want to know the facts, here goes. Like I said I'm Lijuan and I turned sixteen today. I live with my mum in Sydney, but when I was younger we lived in New Zealand and before that we were in Shanghai, although because we left China when I was two I don't really remember that. I go to school up the road, at Newtown High, and I'm good at maths and media but pretty ordinary at anything involving science. What else? I have a best friend, Sash, I play the piano (badly – note to self, practise more) and on weekends I volunteer with one of the reclamation groups. And that's about it. God I sound boring.

SEPTEMBER 27

Came home this afternoon to find Mum back early from work. Turns out her sister in China is sick and she needs to go see her. While she's gone I'm going to stay here on my own.

SEPTEMBER 29

Spent today helping Mum sort things out so she can leave. I don't know how long she'll be gone, although things with my aunt sound bad, and Mum's been talking to people in China pretty much nonstop since she found out.

While she's away I've agreed to do some of her work. Before I was born she trained as a nurse in China, but since we came here she's mostly worked looking after kids and cleaning. For the past few years she's been spending afternoons with a kid called Noah, who lives with his grandfather over near Redfern. I know all about Noah because Mum goes on about him all the time, Noah this and Noah that. Apparently he's on the spectrum, but although he's a bit odd he's also super-bright. His grandfather is some kind of scientist – I met him once and he seemed nice.

Noah's sixteen, like me, and Mum's been looking after him since he was twelve or thirteen. He probably doesn't need to be minded any more but this year she and Noah's grandfather agreed she'd do another year and so she is, but while she's away I'm supposed to be doing it. I'm not sure the whole keeping an eye on Noah thing is really me, but Mum says I have to, so I guess I have to.

OCTOBER 1

First afternoon with Noah. I went early so I could get to know the place and so I was there when he got home. Not sure what I was expecting but he wasn't anything like it. For a start he's Indian, or part-Indian – how Mum managed not to mention that I don't know – and also, weirdly, not bad looking, although he isn't comfortable around people.

He must have known I was going to be there, but when he came in he just acted like I wasn't there until I said hello, then he said hello as well and hurried through to his room.

I know from Mum he spends most of his time in there, reading and working with his data. She says he used to play *Twinmaker*, but he stopped that and now he just reads and hangs out in *Universe* or one of the other virches.

After about an hour I decided I wouldn't see him again, but almost as I did he opened his door and came out into the kitchen. He mumbled a few words about food, but then he just stood there. It took me ages to work out he wanted to get to the fridge and I was in the way, so I stepped aside to let him through. I hadn't noticed it until then but he's super-thin under his clothes. I offered to make him a snack and he sort of lunged at the fridge and told me not to, he'd do it.

I was a bit freaked out after that so I just sat back while he heated noodles. It was funny watching him after hearing Mum talk about him so much, he's not what I expected at all.

OCTOBER 5

Something happened today. Because Mum's in China my feeds have been sending me news items about stuff there, which is good because it means we've got things to talk about besides my aunt when she calls. Usually the stuff is pretty normal, stories about pop stars and politicians, but today there was this weird one about all these people dying in Guangxi. I probably wouldn't have noticed it at all if some other users hadn't promoted it.

Anyway, I tagged it and followed some of the links and it turns out they all seem to have died of some kind of respiratory thing. In the beginning the reports were saying it was flu but by this afternoon they were saying it was actually a virus that hasn't been seen before.

I was pretty freaked out so I pinged Mum. She said she didn't know anything about it but that it was probably nothing. We talked for a while after that, mostly about my aunt, who is getting worse, so Mum's been at the hospital most of the time. Apparently my cousin Jun is coming back from America tomorrow, so it sounds like it may all be heading for some sort of conclusion.

OCTOBER 8

Mum called. Aunty Mei died earlier today. They were all there. We talked for a while and she sounded upset but okay. I don't know how I feel about it, because I didn't really know her, but it still feels weird, like I've lost something I can't describe. The apartment feels very empty just now.

OCTOBER 10

More stories out of China. The government is saying it's just an isolated outbreak, but there are other reports that it's much worse than that. Apparently the area around the outbreak has been closed off, but nobody seems to know whether it has spread. Some people think the government should have reacted faster, but the government just keeps repeating it's under control. I want to ask Mum about it but she's too caught up with Aunty Mei's death. Yesterday when I spoke to her she seemed to think it was okay but today when I pinged her I got no response, and when I try to access her profile it tells me she's offline. I'm not alone either, there are people all over the net complaining they're finding it difficult to contact relatives in China.

OCTOBER 12

Still no word from Mum. I'm sure it's nothing but I wish I could just make sure everything's okay.

OCTOBER 13

I saw Dr Leith today. He came home early. I'd been reading

about the outbreak and when he saw it on my screen he went a little quiet.

'Do you know about it?' I asked, and he just nodded.

'Is it bad?'

'I don't know,' he said. 'We got a bulletin today that made it sound like the Americans and the Europeans are pretty worried.' Then he paused. 'Have you heard from your mum?'

I shook my head. 'Not for four days.'

I could see by his face this wasn't good. 'I'm sure she's fine,' he said.

OCTOBER 15

I'm just writing this quickly. Apparently there are cases in Beijing now. And Shanghai. And Guangzhou. People are saying the Chinese government has been monitoring the traffic and telephones, keeping it under wraps. I've been trying to contact Mum but I still can't get through. It's been a week now and I'm really scared.

OCTOBER 17

The story about the outbreak is all over the place. Everywhere I look there seem to be maps and counters, although nobody really knows what's going on. A lot of people don't believe the figures the Chinese government has released.

A journalist from Canada got into the area of the original outbreak and took some photos and spoke to doctors, who looked frightened and said there were thousands dead. People have been sharing photos and video that are supposed to come from Shanghai and Guangzhou and other places that show people fighting outside hospitals and what look like makeshift clinics in school halls. On the train to Noah's everybody was watching the feeds or texting.

OCTOBER 19

Dr Leith was there again this afternoon, and said he hadn't been to work. When I came in he asked me if I'd seen Noah, and when I said no he closed the door.

'Where are you staying?' he asked.

'At our place,' I said.

'And are you alone or with somebody?'

'Alone.'

He paused in that way he does. 'You still haven't heard from your mum?'

I shook my head. 'No.'

I could see he was thinking about what to say next. 'I'm sure she's fine and this will all blow over. But if I were you I'd stay away from school for a few days. And avoid crowded places.'

'Is it here? In Sydney?'

'I don't know. But it's in Canada and the US and there are reports of cases in the camps in India and Burma.'

'Is it bad?'

'Maybe. They're working on drugs now, and there are detection units at all the airports, but it's already moving.'

I waited until eight to head home so the train would be less crowded. It was emptier than I expected and some people were wearing masks. Nobody talked, they just sat staring at their screens and overlays or looking out the window.

OCTOBER 22

Up all night watching the news. There are hundreds of cases in America now, but still none here. People don't seem able to decide whether to be afraid or not, but if they want to it's got a name now, Acute Viral Respiratory Syndrome, or AVRS. There's data as well. The mortality rate is around 25 per cent, but what's scarier is that the transmission rate seems to be higher again. People are saying its incubation is several days, which is bad because it means it's transmissible before there are symptoms.

There's some maths for it, an equation. Someone has built a simulator online and I played with it for a while and then I got too scared and stopped.

OCTOBER 24

I didn't go to school today, just stayed in the house. There are reports of people panic-buying, filling their cupboards with food, and stories about unrest in the camps up north. There have been more boats, and people are talking about refugees bringing it in with them. One man had pictures of a hospital in Burma, of the bodies outside, and he was showing them to people, saying what if this happens here? It's crazy, like it's all too much – too much information, too many people. It's like we can't control that either, can't keep the stories from spreading. I know I'm just tired but I can't stop thinking about Mum.

OCTOBER 26

It's here. Two cases in Melbourne, three in Sydney.

OCTOBER 28 (morning)

Dr Leith called. He said he's coming to get me. He's got a house up in the north we can go to.

OCTOBER 28 (afternoon)

On the road. Noah is in the front seat, I'm in the back. The weather is hot and grey. Dr Leith says the house is near one of the old national parks and used to belong to his parents, but it got damaged in one of the floods a few years ago.

The road is bad, long queues of cars heading out of the city, people by the side of the road. It's slow and frustrating but Dr Leith doesn't get angry, just sits and stares out the window. Once, a man came and stood by the window screaming, and telling us to fuck off. Dr Leith pressed the lock down and kept staring ahead.

OCTOBER 28 (evening)

We're at the house. I wouldn't have known it was here if I hadn't been shown. It didn't come up on any overlays either. You get to it by a track that runs off a road through the national park, and then up another track to a gate.

The house is small and old but comfortable enough. Dr Leith said it was built back in the teens or twenties, and although it must have been pretty schmick then it's looking faded now. He said they used to come up here most summers, but for the past few years it's been too difficult. A lot of the forest is flooded whenever it rains and there's malaria and cholera around.

There was power when we arrived, from the panels on the roof, but the house smelled damp inside, mildewy, and there was a foul smell coming from the kitchen. Noah covered his face with one hand, he hates strong smells, but

Dr Leith just started opening the windows to air it out.

'We can clean up in the morning,' he said. 'For now let's try to get some sleep.'

It was only then that we noticed someone had been here. There were tins levered open and a dried-up pot on the stove. Dr Leith went still when he saw them, then gestured to us not to say anything.

He went back through to the bedrooms, flicked on the lights and checked them one by one. When he was done he came back to the kitchen.

'Probably just kids,' he said, but I knew from the way he wouldn't look at me he was thinking the same thing I was, which was what would kids be doing out here in the forest?

OCTOBER 29

It was light when I woke up. Dr Leith was in the kitchen with Noah, scanning the feeds on his screen. When he saw me he put it away, which I suppose was sweet but annoyed me at the time.

'What's happening?' I asked and he opened his hand.

'It's everywhere,' he said. 'We did the right thing getting out.'

I knew he wanted to talk to me about Mum, so I went over to look out the window. At some point a storm must have blown through, uprooting trees and sending them tumbling to the forest floor, but the trunks that lay here and there were already disappearing beneath ferns and climbers.

We spent the morning washing the bedding and airing the place out, which took forever because all we had was a few rags, an old broom and an ancient mop, and everything's so wet nothing dries, but once we were done I went for a walk.

I didn't really know where to go, but then, where the clear space around the house ended, I noticed a track running off and followed it. It was narrow, and sometimes seemed to vanish altogether, but I managed to stay on it.

I'm not used to the forest or trees, and to be honest I found it a bit creepy at first. I suppose once there would have been birds and things through here, but now they're gone it's so quiet all you can hear is the leaves moving in the breeze. Maybe I should have thought it was restful but really it was just weird, I've never heard anything so quiet. Although what was worse was the way now and again I'd hear a crack or a crash, like a branch falling somewhere.

After I'd walked a few hundred metres the ground began to get marshy and the number of fallen trees increased. With less cover the sun was hotter, and I began to sweat.

Eventually the path went up onto a sort of ridge and

turned aside, and I came out into what must once have been a river or a creek, but was now a lake that spread out in all directions, with trees standing in the water.

It was sort of sad, all the trees there in the water, but it was also weirdly beautiful. The water was dark brown – tannin from the eucalypts, Dr Leith told me later – and so still you could see the grass and leaves and branches scattered in the shallows.

I would have stayed there longer, but after a while I began to feel sort of uneasy, like somebody was watching me. Looking around I couldn't see anybody, but then again if there was somebody it would have been dead easy for them to hide. Just like realising people had been in the house last night, it creeped me out a bit, so I decided to head back.

Noah had his lenses on when I got there, his face twitching and his hands opening and closing. I watched him for a while, wondering how long the software agents and AIs would keep running if we all died. Would the games continue on without us? It was a strange thought, all those worlds left empty, waiting, their only inhabitants things of bits and light.

OCTOBER 30

The weirdest thing about all this isn't how messed up it is but how normal it is so much of the time. Now that the house is sort of sorted out it's almost like we're on holidays, except that Mum isn't here and everybody's so far away. But when I sit on the veranda or chat to Noah we could be just killing an afternoon at somebody's house.

I said this to Sash earlier this evening and she screwed up her face and told me I was crazy.

'Stuck up there with that freak Noah and his crazy old granddad? It sounds a bit hillbilly to me,' she said, and I laughed, and so did she except then she got all earnest.

'Seriously,' she said, 'are you sure it's safe? I mean, what do you know about them?'

It was stupid but I didn't quite know what to say.

'You think I should come back?'

Sash glanced sideways, looking at something I couldn't see. 'No,' she said.

'What are you thinking?' I said.

'I'm scared, Lisy,' she said. 'They say they're working on a cure but what if they don't find one?'

'What do your parents say?'

Sash made a face again. 'Mum and Anna keep arguing about it. Anna says it's engineered, that we should buy some of the pharma they're selling, but Mum says that's crazy.'

'And your dads?'

'They have to stay away because Anna says we can't

have more people in the house.'

'But you can still chat?'

'Sure, it's just they're all acting so crazy it scares me. What if Anna's right? What if it is engineered? What if we're all going to die?'

'We're not,' I said. Sash looked unconvinced.

'Have you heard from your mum?'

I shook my head. Sash was about to continue but I held up my hand to stop her. 'I have to go,' I said.

When I went outside Noah was standing on the edge of the veranda looking up at the sky, his lips moving as if he was reciting something under his breath. He didn't have his lenses on but the way he was standing told me he was looking at where the stars would be if we could see them.

'Do you know all their names?' I asked after a while.

He just kept moving his lips, faster if anything. But then he stopped and blinked several times.

'Most of them don't have names,' he said.

'What do you mean?'

'You can't count them,' he said. 'There are too many of them. So they just give them numbers.'

The sky was grey and featureless. It seemed dizzying that there should be so many stars we couldn't even name them all.

'How many are there?'

He seemed to be doing a calculation in his head. 'In the galaxy? About three or four hundred billion.'

'And how many galaxies are there?'

'Hundreds of billions. But we can't count them all either, they're too far away.'

He stood staring upwards, his leg jiggling. I found myself wondering what it must be like to be him, whether he, like me, felt something that was half-wonder, half-sadness at the idea of all those stars, all that time, the vastness of it all.

NOVEMBER 2

We went into town today. I asked to go, but I don't think I'd realised how weird it would be. It was so quiet. Twice I saw dogs loping along beside the road, first a skinny yellow one on its own, then later a group of three, who saw the car and turned aside into a driveway.

We stopped outside a convenience store. It looked closed, and despite the security mesh that covered them one of the windows had been broken, and patched up with cardboard and tape. Dr Leith stared at it and then turned to say he thought we should wait in the car.

'I want to come in,' said Noah.

'No. I don't want the two of you taking chances.'

'But you can?' Noah asked.

Before Dr Leith could reply I leaned forward. 'I want to come as well,' I said.

Dr Leith gave me a sharp look then caught himself. 'All right,' he said. 'If you insist. Just don't touch anything. And make sure you keep your masks on.'

It was weird being in a shop after five days in the bush. Familiar and unfamiliar at the same time. Before we arrived I'd thought it would be nice to be able to wander about and look, but once we were inside it was clear the place had been stripped of almost anything anybody might want. While Dr Leith talked to the store owner I picked up a few of the things that remained, looking for stuff that might be useful. It was only when I glanced out through the front window that I saw Noah had gone back out and was standing in the car park.

He had his lenses on but when I approached him he turned.

'Don't you want anything?' I asked.

He shook his head. 'What do you think's going to happen?' he asked.

'Now? I think the plan is to try to buy some food.'

At my words he seemed to close in on himself. 'It's not

funny,' he said. 'We can't stay here forever.'

'They'll find a cure,' I said.

'And if they don't?'

I didn't know the answer to that. 'Then it'll end anyway, I guess. It's just a lot more people will die.'

Noah stood looking at me and I thought I realised what it might be like to be him, to be so alone, and so afraid.

NOVEMBER 3

Still no word from Mum. I've been trying so hard not to think about her, not to worry, but it's really difficult. The media ban is still in place in China but the images that are getting out are bad: hospitals overflowing, bodies in the streets. It's the same all over Asia, and in America and Europe. Until now I've been worried she might be sick, but it could be worse than that, she could be dead, her body dumped in some mass grave or lying in the open somewhere. Some of the big tech companies have been working with the UN to consolidate the information that's flowing in from different countries, so there's a database with details of the dead that people can search if they're worried about friends or relatives, but with so many sick and dying it's impossible to know how accurate the data is. And so I just keep searching and hoping, willing myself to believe she's okay.

NOVEMBER 5

Today I tried something. I've been thinking about what it must have been like out here before the change began, what the forest was like when there were still birds, so I called up a simulation in my overlays and walked out among the trees to listen. The noise was incredible. Birds shrieking and singing, things moving in the undergrowth. Even the light was different, thicker somehow, full of smoke and colour. It was so amazing I didn't realise Noah was nearby until I heard a footstep right behind me, and flicking off my overlays found him standing there.

'Noah!' I said. 'You frightened me.' But as usual he didn't reply, just stood staring at the ground.

'How long have you been there?' I asked. Looking down I saw his hands were clenched. 'Did you want to talk to me?' I asked, more gently this time.

He shook his head, his whole body swaying slightly as he did. 'What are you watching?' he asked at last.

'It's a simulation of what it used to be like here before the birds died. Do you want to see it?'

He gave a stiff nod. I pinged the details across and saw his eyes flicker behind his lenses as he pulled the simulation up. Then an expression of perplexity passed over his face, and once again I was struck by what a space alien he is, how thin and alone. We must all seem very baffling to him. What's it really like being in there, wanting to connect but not knowing how? So many things that seem normal to me must seem almost impossible to him. Without thinking, I took his hand. He recoiled at my touch but then he relaxed.

'It's going to be okay,' I said, and I realised I wanted it to be okay for him as much as for me.

NOVEMBER 8

These are the things we've lost:

> *Birds*
> *Bananas*
> *Tigers*
> *Frogs*
> *Bees*
> *Coffee*
> *Polar bears*
> *Coral*

These are the things we've saved:

> *Seeds*
> *Elephants*
> *Dolphins*
> *Each other*

NOVEMBER 12

I came in today to find Dr Leith crying. Because I thought he hadn't heard me, I was about to slip back to my room when he turned around and told me to stay.

'What's wrong?' I asked.

'A friend,' he said. 'Someone I knew.' Wiping his eyes he looked at me. 'Still nothing from your mum?'

I shook my head. I could see he wanted to say something reassuring but he didn't, and I liked him for not lying to cheer me up.

Then he surprised me by pointing at the fridge and asking, 'Would you like a beer?'

I wasn't sure how to react. Although we've been here for a fortnight now it's still difficult not to feel like I'm only really here because Dr Leith knows my mum and felt bad about leaving me on my own. Plus I'm under-age.

Perhaps he guessed what I was thinking because he said, 'Well, I would.'

'Sure,' I said then, a little too quickly, and he grinned and handed me a bottle.

I followed him out onto the veranda. It was hot and still.

'How are you doing?' he asked.

I took a sip, trying not to screw my face up too much at the taste of it. 'Okay, I suppose.'

'And how do you think Noah's coping?'

'Okay,' I said. 'He's scared.'

Dr Leith took a long draught. 'We all are.'

I hesitated. 'Can I ask you a personal question?'

'Sure. It's not like there's much point in leaving things for later.'

I laughed, and it felt so good, a relief after so long. 'How did you end up looking after Noah?'

'It's a long story. Noah was born in England.'

'Before London?'

'Sometimes when you see the news out of England it's easy to forget it was once a rich country.'

'Was that weird?' I asked. 'Your daughter being so far away?'

'I didn't even know Noah existed until he was seven.'

I must have looked surprised because he smiled in a sad sort of way. 'It's a long story,' he said again.

'Right,' I said. 'And now?'

He didn't answer at once. When he did his voice was different, quieter, almost sad. 'I just want him to be safe. I just want both of you to be safe.'

'You shouldn't worry about me,' I said.

'But I do,' he said.

NOVEMBER 15

I've been watching the feeds and it seems difficult to believe this isn't the end. It's not just that so many people are dead, it's that everything seems to be coming unstitched. In Europe there are gangs on the streets, in America they're closing off cities and killing anybody who tries to get in. Here in Australia groups are taking over suburbs and buildings, trying to quarantine them. The police have been shooting people, and the army are out, but nobody believes they'll be able to control things. And because the net keeps going down nobody can even keep track of all of it any more.

NOVEMBER 18

Noah told me about his mother today. I thought she was dead, but it turns out it's more complicated than that. He was living with her in England when Dr Leith came to visit them. That was right when the first massive flood happened, and although the three of them got through it together, she disappeared straight afterwards. I asked Noah whether she died and he said she didn't die, she just vanished.

I didn't say anything, trying to imagine what that must have been like, and for a long time Noah didn't say anything either, just sat staring at the ground like he always does. For once his leg wasn't jiggling, but you could see the restlessness was still there, straining at him.

'She didn't mean to do it,' he said at last. 'Didn't mean to leave me. Not really. It was just too much, too difficult, and she didn't know what to do.'

When I still didn't say anything he said, 'It's true. She's not a bad person.' His voice was almost angry.

'What does your grandfather think?' I asked.

'I don't know. He never talks about her. It's like he doesn't want me to know about her.'

'I'm sure it's not like that,' I said, but he didn't answer.

NOVEMBER 20

Noah and Dr Leith had an argument today. It was after dinner and I was out the back when I heard a crash. I came in to find Noah standing in the middle of the kitchen with broken glass in front of him.

'Pick it up,' Dr Leith was saying, but Noah shook his head.

'Pick it up,' he said again, but Noah just stared at him.

'Pick it up!' Dr Leith said for a third time. Noah flinched, then pushed past him and ran outside, slamming the screen door. I began to back away, embarrassed, but Dr Leith looked up and saw me. I thought he might say

something, but when he didn't I followed Noah out into the night.

I was pretty sure he'd gone to the lake, so I went down the path through the forest. The sky was full of stars, so bright you could almost feel the Earth moving beneath you.

Noah was down by the water, sitting on a log. I could see his shape against the surface of the lake. He must have heard me approaching but he didn't turn.

'Hey,' I said as I got to him and sat myself down.

He didn't acknowledge my presence.

'Are you okay?' I asked.

Finally he nodded abruptly.

'He doesn't mean it, you know,' I said. 'He's just worried.'

'It's stupid,' he said. 'In a couple of years I'll be able to do what I want, but for now I have to listen to him.'

I laughed and that made him turn towards me briefly.

'What's so funny?'

'You seem to do a pretty good job of doing what you want now,' I said. 'And you spend so much time playing *Universe* and doing your astronomical simulations it's not like you're around all that much anyway.'

'It's easier in there. Less complicated. I can be myself.'

'I know,' I said. 'Out here's confusing for all of us.'

From somewhere in the distance came a rumbling

sound. I thought it was thunder, but then it came again, louder. In the sky to the south a glow was visible.

'What's that?' I asked, but Noah's eyes were already moving behind his lenses.

'A fire in a gas reservoir in Sydney,' he said, and before he could say anything else there was another rumble, louder this time, and the glow grew brighter.

'Jesus,' I said. 'At this rate there may not be any "out here" left for us to find complicated.'

NOVEMBER 22

I've been reading about autism. It's not a subject I've ever thought about very much, and if I had I think I'd assumed it was just some kind of genetic disorder, but it's more complicated than that. To begin with it's not one condition, it's about five or six, all overlapping and interacting. Some have to do with language, others with the development of the bits of the brain that help us understand what other people are feeling, some with processing information.

There are different genes associated with all of these conditions, and they express themselves in different ways. Some people are unable to communicate at all, others have trouble making sense of auditory information, or isolating meaning from noise, others find it difficult to relate and connect to other people.

It must be so hard to live in a world filled with signs and signals you don't understand, with people who do baffling things and expect you to react in particular ways. No wonder people on the spectrum find the modern world so frightening and complicated.

I can see it in Noah, in how alone he often seems. When I first met him I thought he was weird, cut off, but the more time I spend with him, the easier it is to see he has feelings, he just doesn't know how to articulate them, how to control them, so when they come they come in a rush, as anger or frustration. It's like he's a little child sometimes, and all that feeling is backed up, trying to find a way out.

NOVEMBER 25

I'm really frightened. This last week things seem to have gotten rapidly worse. In China and India the cities are burning, death rates are way up, and there's still no sign of a cure. It feels like there won't ever be one, like this is it. Although Dr Leith hasn't said anything I can see he feels the same, and so does Noah. They've been fighting again, which doesn't help, but I think the fighting is partly because they're scared. Sometimes I try to imagine what the world would be like without people, what would happen if we were all gone, and it makes me so sad. The cities are ugly and there are too many of us, but it seems wrong that we should end this way.

NOVEMBER 30

It's late and I should be asleep but I want to get this down while I can. It's been five days since I wrote in here and a lot has happened, most of it bad. The first thing was four days ago when the net went down. The first time it was just a blip, ten minutes without coverage, but then it happened again and we lost it for a few hours, and then for good. Dr Leith says it means there's a problem with the satellite, and the systems can't cope any more, but whatever it is it's really scary, because we only have occasional coverage from a local node.

But that was only the beginning. Although we didn't realise it at the time, the explosion the other night wasn't an accident, and reports have been coming in ever since about rioting and looting and fires. Dr Leith says the situation has reached a sort of tipping point, and things are beginning to fall apart too quickly for anybody to stop them.

To make things worse, he and Noah have been fighting constantly. It's awful. Not just because it makes me feel like I shouldn't be here, but because I can see neither of them want to fight, they just don't seem to be able to stop.

This morning it was over Noah saying we have to head back into town to get food and Dr Leith not wanting us to. Noah accused him of being afraid, said he'd always been afraid, and that he wanted to keep Noah from ever doing anything. Dr Leith said that wasn't it, he was trying to keep us all safe, and it wasn't safe in town. Noah was angry and upset, which is always difficult to watch because he seems to go all stiff, as if he's about to explode.

'Please, Noah,' Dr Leith said at last, 'we can't keep doing this.'

'You did this to her as well, didn't you?' Noah said. 'That's why she left, why she left me.'

Dr Leith went so still and pale that I thought he was going to hit Noah. But when he spoke again his voice was very quiet and very careful, which was somehow even worse.

'I'm sorry you feel that way,' he said.

Afterwards I tried to talk to him but he waved me away. 'I don't want to discuss it,' he said. 'We've said enough.'

When I went out to look for Noah he had his lenses on.

'Is the net back up?' I asked.

'There's a backlink but it's weak.'

'Is there any news?'

Noah shook his head. I sat down beside him.

'Do you think you'd know?' he asked after a moment.

'Know what?'

'If your mother was dead?'

I felt something catch in my throat. Then I realised he was looking at me. 'I don't know,' I said. 'Sometimes I tell myself I would have to know, that it isn't possible for her to be gone without me knowing it. It's stupid, because so many people have died, but I just can't imagine the world without her, can't believe she could be gone.'

I felt my voice crack and I had to fight to hold back tears. Next to me Noah was staring at the ground in front of him.

'What about you? Do you think you'd know?' I asked.

'Before we came here, before everyone got sick, I always told myself I would. But now I don't know. Everything is all wrong.'

I put my hand on his. This time he didn't flinch. I could smell his sharp funky smell, the rubber of his sneakers. Not knowing what else to do I leaned over, pulled his head towards me, tears coming in a gasp.

DECEMBER 2

Dr Leith woke us when the fire began and told us to get dressed. If he was surprised to find us in the same bed he didn't say anything, although he looked at me in a way he hadn't before, like he was disappointed. As Noah put his clothes on I thought about going after his grandfather and trying to explain that it wasn't how it looked, that we both just needed to know there was somebody nearby, but I wasn't sure it would make any difference.

Out on the road the glow of the fire was visible to the west, and as we drove I watched it against the sky.

'Where are we going?'

Dr Leith glanced around at me. 'The coast. We should be okay there.'

From behind us I could feel the heat coming in gusts and judders. In the darkness beside me Noah had gone quiet.

'You don't need to worry,' Dr Leith said. 'The fire's a long way off. We've got lots of time.'

'What about the house?' Noah asked.

'With any luck it'll be fine,' Dr Leith replied. When Noah didn't answer he said, 'Besides, I thought you hated it.'

'I do,' Noah said. 'I just don't want it to burn.'

Dr Leith smiled. 'Neither do I,' he said as we rounded the head and the ocean came into view. To the east the moon was huge and pale and shimmered on the water. Dr Leith pulled in and we climbed out, the sand thick and coarse and yellow beneath our feet.

'We're here,' he said.

ECHO

I'm not sure what makes the order stand out. Some detail in the description, perhaps. Or the fact that it's a child. Not that that's unusual, of course: a lot of our orders are children. But something about it catches my eye as I'm flicking through the assignments, making me pause long enough to realise I recognise the face in the photo accompanying it.

He's older than he was the last time I saw him, five or six rather than three or four. But even without reading the details I know it's him. Cassie's little brother. Matthew.

It shouldn't come as a surprise, I suppose; there are so many who died, after all. But somehow it does. I haven't thought about either of them for quite a while, although like a lot of us I think I've learned not to dwell too much upon people we've lost contact with, or to ask too many questions. But still, as I scan the order I'm relieved to find it's in her name, even if there's no mention of other family.

Exiting the order, I call up my logs, pull up a picture of her. Her face so familiar, so far away.

We're supposed to report orders like this, of course, to prevent situations in which people might feel their privacy has been invaded. But as I look at Matthew's photo I'm seized by the thought that I can help somehow, make it better than it would be otherwise, the idea so clear I scarcely notice myself tagging the job as my own.

They're called sims, or echoes. Virtual recreations of the dead assembled from photos and videos. Back before the pandemic they were pretty rare. Sometimes people created sims of themselves when they got old or sick, hoping they might live on; occasionally they were bought by parents or spouses prostrate with grief. But mostly they were seen as slightly grotesque rather than consoling.

Since the pandemic, though, it's as if for every person who would rather forget there is another who cannot bear to let go, who needs the past to continue. And so they come to Semblance and other companies like us, wanting us to recreate those who have been lost.

They're not the person, of course, even if it's often difficult to tell the difference. Instead they're copies programmed with as much information about the originals as we can get. At their core is a cloned, virtual Artificial Intelligence, programmed with heuristics that allow it to read the responses of people it interacts with so it can mimic the dead person as closely as possible. They're not conscious, or not quite: they're complex emulations fully focused on convincing their owners they are who they seem to be.

Or at least that's the theory. In reality a lot of people who order sims are after quite specific things. They want them to remember a certain holiday, but not like that, like this. Or to be more grateful, or full of praise. I've heard stories about sims being programmed to apologise, or to enumerate the ways in which they failed or hurt the people who've ordered them. It's a bit creepy but it's hardly surprising: after all, if you could recreate a family member exactly as they were, would you want to? Or would you rather rewire them a bit, make them the way you always wanted them to be?

I don't program the AIs; my job is to help get the facial expressions and mannerisms right. This is important, because although the software is good at guessing what people looked like when they were alive and at helping the sims to emote, it's not perfect. Back in the early years of the century they used to call it the uncanny valley, that space where a robot became so close to lifelike that it began to terrify us, not because it was perfect but because it wasn't quite. There was a theory that this fear was instinctive, a fight or flight response to something outside the realm of our experience, generated by a deep cognitive dissonance. The same thing happens with the sims: no matter how good the systems are at copying, they never get it quite right. And that's where I come in. My job is to find the imperfections, the little details the software misses. To put the grit in the oyster.

I got the work by accident. Before Mum died, before the pandemic, I used to spend a lot of time in the virches. There was a group of us who hacked avatars, and pulled pranks on people we thought deserved it. It was kids' stuff, really, sticking new faces on characters and generally messing about. But then some agent or other took notice and gave my details to Semblance, who offered me a job.

It's a good gig. Semblance operates out of Guangzhou, although most of us work remotely, so I'm not stuck in an office somewhere. And I enjoy the work, not just because of the money, but because people's faces fascinate me: the way they sometimes seem to have two expressions at once, one showing emotion, one trying to hide it, the unintentional ways they reveal us. I love looking for the flicker that comes before someone registers what's going on, for those moments where you can see the unconscious mind working faster than the conscious. That's how we know somebody's really there, by seeing emotions move through them, by seeing the times when they're not there, or not quite.

I spend the rest of the afternoon reviewing the data. Because he was only six when he died it's mostly photos and videos, but there are also a lot of excerpts from Cassie's lifelogs. I don't need to watch them all – the systems will analyse them as they assemble the information for his sim – but as the day slips away I pull up more and more. Although most of them are of Matthew, there are videos of her as well, laughing or posing for the camera. And sometimes, in the background, a glimpse of myself.

It's always slightly weird watching lifelogs and ambient video. Not because they capture the moment, but because of the way the past seems to hover, just out of reach, both close at hand and already lost. Watching her, watching him, my memory of the time I spent with the two of them is so vivid, yet the person I was, the one who had no idea what lay just ahead, seems like a stranger.

I'm so absorbed in what I'm doing that I'm still at it around ten when Dad's bike comes crunching up the drive. I know he's in a mood without seeing him. These past months he's been doing odd jobs, helping people out for a few dollars here and there, but it isn't easy, and it isn't like it was before. It probably doesn't help that I make enough money for both of us, so he doesn't have to work at all and we don't have to worry about ending up on the road or in one of the camps, but I sometimes wonder whether it'd be like this anyway.

He leaves his bike by the back door and after opening the fridge in the kitchen goes through to the living room. After that it falls quiet, so I assume he must have turned on his screen or lenses until I hear his voice behind me.

'You hungry?'

Minimising my overlays I turn. Once he was handsome, in a slightly rough kind of way. Now he just looks tired and dirty. And old.

'Not really,' I say.

'Have you eaten?' He glances around my room. 'Have you left here at all today?'

'Sure,' I lie.

'There's pizza in the kitchen.'

'Great,' I say. 'I'll get some in a bit.'

He seems to be waiting for me to say more, and when I don't he turns away.

'I'm going to bed,' he says.

Once he's gone I open the files again, but I've lost the thread. Dad dislikes me doing this work, he thinks it's exploitative. But I know that's not his real problem with it.

I'm not sure when he got so angry. Partly it's about Mum, but it's more than that. It's like he's caught, and he doesn't know what to do. And being with me just seems to make it worse.

He wasn't always like this. Before the economy collapsed he worked on a solar farm in the desert up north. He was just a casual maintenance guy but he had a scooter to get around the facilities, and some nights he would take me with him and ride me out to the collectors. It got cold at night up there, so there was something reassuring about being with him, about the heat from the panels radiating out into the dark. Sometimes when I'm really lonely I think about those nights, about the hum of the scooter, the smell of the air.

Looking at the images of Matthew I find myself wondering whether he had a place like that, a time he remembered. Although I've already read it half a dozen times I call up the brief again, try to put my finger on whatever it is I cannot quite pin down. The brief says he is six but I would have guessed four. After a while I realise it isn't him I'm looking at, but her. What happened after they left? I find myself wondering. I said I'd stay in touch but we'd been broken up for six months by then, and while we messaged each other once or twice I don't think either of us was really bothered when we dropped out of contact.

Eventually I fire off a message to one of my old classmates, Hugo.

Looking at old pictures. Do you remember Cassie Meek?

It's been a while since Hugo and I were in contact so I'm surprised when he replies almost immediately.

Your Cassie?

Not sure she'd like you to call her that, but yes.

Of course. I thought she died.

No, she's alive. Did you stay in touch with her after she moved away?

I imagine Hugo seated in his room as he ponders this. *Not really. I think some of the others did.*

Who?

Rhianna, maybe. Jaya. The Sailor twins.

Looking at their names, the faces of the Sailor twins and Jaya come to me unbidden. Other than Mum, I try not to think about the people who are gone. It's the only way, this forgetting.

Thanks, I type. Then after a moment I add, *You okay?*

There's a lag, which might be nothing or might be exactly what it feels like.

Sure, man. I'm good.

The conversation with Hugo over, I go back to the brief and begin work. The emulation engine is an M417, one of our cheaper models, probably bought from one of the discount wholesalers who resell our packages. The software has done quite a good job on Matthew's sim, though: watching him he looks almost human. But not quite.

Ordinarily what I do now is pretty standard. I don't need to worry about the sim's conversation because the heuristics will improve that over time, but I have a few tricks that help. Incorporate some sub-routines to make them look like they're sitting on a joke, or thinking good thoughts about you before they speak; splice in a hesitation here and there; insert a routine so that just occasionally you'll catch them looking at you when they think you can't see them, which will help create a subliminal connection by reassuring your subconscious mind that they don't just shut down when you're not looking at them.

All of that's more difficult with kids. Some of the people who program sims think this is because children wear their emotions so much closer to the surface than adults, cycling through them so quickly and transparently, and a lot of packages emphasise that – their kids are labile little love machines. But the real reason kids are difficult is because they're so inward. If you don't know what I mean, watch some: you'll see how much of their time is spent engaged with whatever it is they're doing, trying things out, becoming themselves. The things most people remember about them – the moments their kids hug them or say they love them – aren't the real kids. The real them is the version that's moving on, leaving their parents behind.

Some systems are designed to emulate that, so as time passes the sims grow older and change, but you can only guess at the way people will age. So usually they're programmed to age more slowly than in real life, or they just stay the same, like ghosts. Which seems even sadder somehow.

Looking at Matthew I try to remember what he was like when I knew him. Funny, filled with life, obsessed with dinosaurs and superheroes. But beyond that I struggle, because to me at least he was just another little kid. And so I do what I always do: I speculate and imagine and fill in the details.

It's almost five before I decide to stop for the night. From the kitchen I can hear Dad snoring in the next room. Outside the wind is up, sweeping down from the hills to the north, and in the backyard the turbines creak and turn, the lights flickering occasionally as the system tries to regulate the flow.

Before Mum died it never felt lonely out here. Even with the heat and the silence it was a good place. But now she's not here any more it's different. I suppose lots of places are – the death toll was so high – but with just me and Dad it's difficult not to feel as if we're stuck here, that if we leave we'll be leaving her behind.

I'm so deep in thought I don't realise Dad has woken up until he steps through the door behind me.

He is tired and pale. 'You're still up?'

'I've been working,' I say. 'I'm sorry if I woke you.'

He ignores my apology. 'I think the turbines are playing up again,' he says, looking up at the lights. 'I need to take a look at them tomorrow.'

'Sure,' I say, then realise he might have meant for me to volunteer to help him. 'I could help, if you want.'

'I'll be fine,' he says.

A lot of people still want answers about where the virus came from. Some say it escaped from a lab in Taiwan, or in what was left of the Netherlands. Others say they have evidence it was released by one of the numerous terrorist groups that claimed responsibility when it first began to spread. Still others argue it was just a natural occurrence, the odds falling against us. I'm not sure I really care: after all, it's not like knowing where it came from will make it unhappen or bring anybody back to life. What's done is done, what matters now is finding some way to pick up the pieces and carry on.

Maybe I wouldn't feel like that if Mum hadn't died. She didn't get sick until right near the end, only a few days before they announced they'd found the antibodies and sent the details to the fabricators. The stupid thing was that we'd been really careful through the early stages – although we lived far enough out of town for the risk of casual infection to be low we'd decided to stay inside as much as possible, and to make sure we wore gloves and masks when we went out for food.

Of course none of that guaranteed we'd be safe. There were stories about gangs of people looting houses left empty by the sickness, or killing those who remained. One night Dad woke up screaming and I thought we were being attacked, but when I went in there was nobody there, just Dad standing in the door to the bathroom and Mum seated on the side of the bed.

I couldn't sleep again that night, or not until after the sun was up. We were all scared, it felt like the world was ending and there was nothing we could do about it. And so I put my lenses on, went walking in one of the virches. Back then I spent a lot of time in *Universe*, and although a lot of the people I knew there had disappeared, I still went there, sometimes to play, more often just to wander through the worlds. I fetched up on a moon around a gas giant in a system on the edge of the Rift, a place where gardens grew on gleaming towers and the great sphere of the planet and its rings filled the sky.

Afterwards it was difficult not to wonder whether Dad's dream was a premonition of some sort, because a few days later I came into the front hall to find Mum staring out the window. It was a hot day, and while the sky was grey and heavy the UV was so strong you had to squint, even inside. She looked frightened.

'What is it?' I asked, and she gestured out the window.

At first I didn't see anything, then I noticed somebody kneeling by the gate. A woman, dark-haired and thin.

'What's she doing?' I asked.

'She's got two kids with her,' Mum said. As she spoke the woman stood up and turned to face the house. The window was tinted but the way she stood there made me certain she knew the two of us were watching her.

After several seconds she seemed to reach some kind of decision, and began to walk up the drive. It was only then that I realised she was sick.

'Wait here,' Mum said, her tone telling me she meant it, and opening the door she stepped out. Whether out of regard for our safety or because she hadn't quite summoned the courage to take us on, the woman stopped when she saw Mum.

'You can't come in here,' Mum said.

The woman was small, her dark skin ashen and sweaty. 'Please,' she said. 'I need help. My children . . .'

I saw Mum hesitate. The kids were standing by the gate, watching.

'No,' she said. 'We can't. You have to go somewhere else.'

'The hospital is full,' the woman said, taking a step closer. 'And if I take them there they'll get sick as well.'

Mum shook her head, but I could see she was finding it difficult to insist. 'You need to keep moving,' she said in a low voice.

'Just them,' the woman said. 'Please. They're not sick.'

'No —' Mum began, but before she could finish, the woman lunged forward and grabbed her by the wrist.

'Please,' she said, 'you have to help them. You have to.'

Mum cried out, trying to break the woman's grip, but

she wouldn't let go. I charged out to try to intervene, but Mum screamed at me to get back inside. The woman was on her knees now, crawling after Mum as she tried to get free, babbling and crying until finally Mum threw her arms up in a convulsive movement that sent the woman sprawling on the ground. 'Go,' Mum yelled at her. 'Get out of here.'

Once in the house she leaned against the front door, staring at the arm the woman had grabbed. I began to speak but she lifted a hand to silence me.

'Stay away from me,' she said, backing past me to the bathroom.

She was still in there when Dad got home. He'd been out looking for food and I think he knew something was wrong before he got in the door.

'What's happened?' he asked. I started to explain, and as I did the blood drained out of his face. Advancing on the bathroom door, he leaned against it and called Mum's name.

'Don't come in,' she said in a small voice from behind the door. 'It's not safe.'

That day passed slowly. Dad did his best, but it was obvious he was frightened, and frustrated.

While he paced around I tried to stay out of his

way. I knew Mum was right to keep clear of us – all the information emphasised that the virus was transmissible by touch as well as the transfer of bodily fluids – but still it didn't seem right that she was in there alone.

Late in the afternoon she told us to go into the kitchen and close the door; once we were in there I heard her open the bathroom door and go down the hall to the spare room. Dad looked at me as that door closed, then the two of us followed her down.

'Have you got everything you need?' Dad asked her, his face against the door. 'Do you need food?'

'Go over to the Nguyens',' she said. 'See if they've got any masks and gloves.'

I could see Dad wanted to argue, to say he should stay. But instead he said, 'I'll be back as soon as I can.' Then he looked at me and said, 'Call me if anything happens. Anything.'

I told him I would, and listened to him run outside and down the drive. I think I understood my mother had sent him to the Nguyens' because she knew he needed to be occupied. Alone now I sat down against the wall beside the door. From inside I heard my mother's voice.

'Is that you, Dylan?' she asked.

I tried to answer but my voice cracked. On the other side of the door I could hear her breathing. When at last she spoke again her voice was low, and it sounded as if she'd been crying.

'I wonder what happened to those kids,' she said.

It's almost three in the afternoon when I'm woken by the sound of Dad in the drive. Pulling back the curtain I see him standing by the turbines in the backyard, toolbox at his feet.

Watching him I'm reminded how capable he is with tools and machines. There's an economy and certainty to the way he approaches the tasks he takes on that often seems at odds with his manner the rest of the time.

Pulling on a T-shirt I head out into the yard, screwing up my eyes against the glare.

'Hi,' I say. He glances around but doesn't reply.

'Have you figured out what's wrong with them?'

He tugs on a spanner. 'I'm not sure. They need oiling but there's a problem with the inverter as well.'

'Is that why we've been getting power fluctuations?'

'Probably.'

Before I was born, when Mum and Dad were first together, they'd go to the events out in the desert. Back then the economy hadn't completely collapsed, and people used to build sculptures so big you could probably have seen them from space. There are still vids of the pair of them from then, not much older than I am now, dressed in costumes and laughing and dancing. Looking at Dad now I wonder whether he ever imagined this would be how things ended up.

'I spoke to Hugo,' I say.

Dad grunts. I wait for a moment or two then continue. 'I've got a job for Cassie Meek.'

At this he lowers his spanner and looks at me. 'Cassie Meek from school?'

'It's a sim of Matthew.'

'Her brother?'

I nod.

'Is that ethical? Given you know her?'

'It came to me by accident. I wanted to do it.'

'Does Cassie know you're doing it?'

I shake my head.

'You have to send it back.'

'No,' I say, 'I can't. Anyway it's too late, it's nearly finished.'

'It's exploitative.'

'No one makes people buy them.'

'That's not the point. It's preying on people, taking their money when they're vulnerable.'

'It makes them happy.'

'Bullshit. It's wrong.' He is angry now. 'And if it's so okay, why haven't you told her you're working on it, messing around with her memories?'

I start to answer but I can't find the words, so instead we stand there staring at each other, the turbine creaking gently beside us, until finally I turn around and walk back to the house. As I reach the door he calls out, 'Dylan, wait!' but I ignore him and go inside.

It takes two more days to finish Matthew's sim. As always there are patches when I lose myself in the task, certain the work I'm doing is good, or better than good, but this time those moments are shadowed by something else, a feeling more like anger. Or shame.

Once I'm done I send the files back. Usually that's the end of it, but today I make sure I keep a copy of the master code so I can continue to access the system. And then, finally, I go to bed, and sleep.

It's still early when I wake, but already hot outside. In his bedroom Dad is still sleeping; as I leave I pause outside his room, pull the door shut as quietly as I can.

Normally I'd ride my bike to the station but this

morning I decide to walk. Back before things started to go topsy, this area was laid out as a kind of satellite suburb. Things must have gone wrong, and although some of the houses were finished a lot of them were left empty.

After Dad lost his job at the solar farm we needed somewhere to live, and this place had the advantage of being cheap. It wasn't terrible either, at least when I was younger, even if we were always being warned not to play in the empty buildings. But since the pandemic and New York and all the rest of it, people have been leaving, heading back to the city or further out in search of somewhere they could grow things.

By the time I reach the station it's 9:30 and the sun is so bright it makes my eyes hurt. Taking a seat I stare at the water of the gulf to the west, still and shimmering in the morning light, its shattering blue tinged here and there with the rusty blotches of algae blooms, and try to distract myself from what lies ahead.

Everybody knew by then that the incubation period was approximately seventy-two hours, which meant we had three days to wait before we knew whether Mum was infected, three days that passed impossibly slowly. With all of us in the house it was impossible to quarantine her completely, but we did our best, using separate bathrooms and only talking through the door.

On the third night I lay awake for a long time, listening for her cough or a cry. I knew that if she made it through the night the odds were good that she had avoided infection. Eventually I heard her turn off her light, and some time after that I fell asleep, but a few hours later I woke to the sound of coughing. In the hall the door to the spare room was open, and inside Dad was kneeling by her bed, a mask and gloves on, one hand on her forehead.

The address Cassie gave when she signed up is in one of the southern suburbs. I don't know the area but I don't know the city well anyway, so that's not saying much. Thankfully the train line passes through it, so once I've done the two-hour stop-start from our place I set off to walk the last kilometre or so.

The houses and flats are run-down, the wide streets mostly empty. Here and there on the corners people have posted pictures of the dead and left flowers or toys; with the naked eye they look shabby and faded, sheets of curling paper shifting in the wind, but with lenses on they're almost overwhelming, the videos and photos tagged to them creating shifting, entreating jumbles of voices and faces, all moving and laughing and talking, oblivious to what is coming for them.

Cassie's place is in an old block of flats, a cream-brick building from the twentieth century. There's no security so I just walk up and knock on her door.

She looks the same and different. Her hair is longer, and her arms and face are tanned, as if she has been working outdoors. But she also seems older, and somehow very far away from the Cassie I knew. Perhaps I look different as well because she doesn't seem to recognise me. Then her mouth opens.

'Dylan? What are you doing here?'

I remember how we were when we were together. It seems so long ago.

'Can I come in?' I ask.

She leads me into the living room. Some of the furniture is new but I recognise a couple of things from her mum's house. I can see she is flustered, uncertain why I'm here.

'How did you find me?' she asks.

'It's a long story.'

'How have you been?'

'Okay.'

'And your parents?'

'Dad's okay. Mum . . .'

When I don't finish she touches my hand. 'Oh Dylan,' she says. 'I'm sorry.'

'Thank you,' I say. For a moment neither of us speaks, then I ask if I can sit down.

'Of course,' she says, 'please.'

I ask her questions then. About what she's doing, where she's been. Her mum and Matthew came down with the virus early on, and soon afterwards she got sick as well. By the time she was well enough to know what was happening they were both gone, so she decided to stay on and work at the hospital with some of the other survivors. After that she picked up a job in one of the gardens, which is where she's been ever since. Although she doesn't say so I think there must be a boyfriend.

Despite this, we seem to fall straight back into the way we were when we were together. It's been three years since we saw each other, and it's pretty clear we've both changed, but it's still there, that bond.

It's only after I've been there half an hour that I tell her why I've come.

'I've got a job too,' I say.

She smiles. 'Really?'

'Making sims,' I reply.

It takes a moment for what I've said to register. Then she looks away.

'Oh,' she says. Then, more quietly, 'Oh.'

'There's nothing to be ashamed of.'

'It was stupid,' she says, still not looking at me.

'You miss him,' I say. 'Why is it stupid to want to remember him?'

'I can't really afford it,' she says. 'It was a subscription deal.'

Most of the sim purchase plans are subscription-based, but I don't tell her that.

'You don't know what it's been like, not having him.' She shudders, as if she is about to cry. 'And before you say it, I know it's dumb. He was just a kid, just one kid, and so many people lost loved ones. But it's like I can't get past it. Sometimes it's all I think about. Having him here. The way he was.'

'I understand,' I say. I touch her arm and she turns to look at me.

'Do you?'

'Really.'

'Have you made one of your mum?'

I begin to tell her that Dad won't let me, but then I

realise it's more than that. Why won't I make a sim of Mum? I could do a good one, after all, so good it would be hard to tell it wasn't real. I could program it myself, give it all her little tics, all her memories. And I'm not vain enough to think I'd be able to resist believing it was real a lot of the time, accepting it as a person. But in the end it wouldn't *be* her, it would be a copy, and somehow that would be even worse than her being gone.

'Because we can't go back,' I say at last.

She nods. 'Are you here to tell me you cancelled my order?'

'No,' I say. 'The opposite, in fact. I brought it so you could see it.'

Mum died less than twenty-four hours after she got sick. It all happened so quickly she barely woke up again. Despite the risk Dad and I stayed to the end, holding her hand, trying to keep her fever down. For a while we thought we might get lucky, that she might be one of those who pulled through, but she grew weaker and weaker, until she slipped away just before dusk.

The quarantine regs required people to place the dead out for collection but the trucks had stopped coming weeks before, so the next morning Dad went out and dug a grave under the old gum at the back of the house, driving the shovel into the ground over and over. And when he was done we wrapped her in a sheet and carried her out there together. I don't think either of us knew what to say, and so we just knelt there next to each other, Dad's arm around my shoulders. It seemed impossible to me that she was in that hole, that she was gone.

Seated next to each other on the sofa Cassie and I activate our lenses. I enter the master code to access Semblance's systems and the sim appears in front of us. He is wearing a Batman outfit, just like he used to, and in one hand he clutches a toy dinosaur. He lifts the dinosaur and roars. Cassie gives a little gasp.

'Is he old enough?' I ask, and she nods quickly, fiercely.

'Can I talk to him?'

'Of course.'

Leaning forward she clasps her hands together. 'Matthew?'

He turns to face her.

'Do you recognise me?' she asks.

'Of course,' he says, rolling his eyes. 'You're Cassie.'

'That's right,' she says in a trembling voice. 'I'm Cassie.'

She looks at me. 'Is he real? On the inside?'

I nod. 'He thinks he is.'

She turns back to the sim, her hands tight in her lap. He stands watching her. Then he grins.

'You want to see my dinosaur fly?' he asks.

Cassie nods. 'Sure,' she says. 'I'd like that.'

The sim grins delightedly and lifts the hand holding the dinosaur high. Then with a roar he turns and spins away.

Next to me Cassie sits very still, her eyes full of tears. 'Look at him,' she says. 'He's so happy.'

I take her hand. On the other side of the room the sim roars again, and whirling the dinosaur ahead of him charges out of sight around the corner.

1420 MHz

1

Sometimes at night the sky so deep he thinks he might fall, tumble upwards into that cold immensity of space, of time. The feeling like vertigo.

Like flight.

2

Lifting his eyes to the window he realises it has grown dark. Last time he looked it was still dusk, the sky fading orange and red, but now all that is visible is blackness, the reflected image of the hospital room. Surprised, he wonders how long it is since he last looked up: ordinarily he would know instinctively, but in these past days and hours space and time seem to have altered, the world contracting until it is only this room, the sound of her breath, the minutes stretching out to infinity, asymptotic. Catching his image in the glass he is struck by the realisation that this is how we live as well, our movement towards those around us like a long arc growing ever closer but never touching, the desire to tell her sharp, like grief. In the bed beside him she breathes in again, the air rasping in her throat; reaching out he takes her hand, closes it in his.

3

In the car park beside the main building he stops and climbs out into the heat, the taste of dust thick in his mouth. Blinking against the brightness he looks around, taking in the familiar bulk of the control centre, the low line of the residential units and common area off to the east. Even close up they are deserted, their prefab structures bleached and battered by the sun.

On the far side of the car park the door to the control centre swings open and the figure of Jin emerges, his wide-boned face obscured behind dark lenses.

'Noah!' he calls out as he jogs over. 'You're late!'

Noah shuffles his feet and looks at the ground. 'The plane was late.'

Jin laughs. 'We know. We checked.' He gestures towards the building. 'Shall we get inside?'

After the heat of the car park the cool of the

air-conditioned interior is restful, almost soporific.

'Do you want to head over to your unit and dump your bag? Or shall we go through to the control room?'

'The control room,' Noah says. 'I want to get started.'

As they step into the room several others look around or wave in greeting. Awkwardly Noah waves back, relieved to see that the technician he has always found most difficult is absent. Jin is explaining the arrangements for that evening's scans while he directs Noah to the desk he has been assigned, but Noah's mind is already elsewhere.

As a student he learned to love the control rooms of observatories. The first time he entered one he felt as if he were stepping into a hallowed space, a place in which it was possible to lose himself in communion with the beyond. In time he learned to love them for other things as well – their quiet, their solitude and order, the sense that those around him were united by a shared fascination with the stars, meaning he didn't have to explain himself or answer questions. Even now he finds something calming about control rooms, about knowing he is connected to the silent immensity of the sky.

'You're sorted then?' Jin asks.

Noah gives a tight nod and Jin smiles.

'It's good to have you back, Noah.'

4

It is five years since he first came here. On that visit he flew from Sydney to Perth then took a solar glider up the coast to Exmouth. He had planned to read but found he couldn't. Instead he sat by the window watching the land unspool beneath him, the seemingly endless patchwork of red and grey and dirty green, scarred here and there by the pale spread of salt and floodlines.

He had been outside the city before, of course. But it wasn't until the glider landed and he walked out of the tiny terminal that it really came home to him how far away he was from everywhere else. As his car angled itself out onto the highway and began the long drive north, the emptiness almost palpable. From the plane, thunderclouds had been visible over the Indian Ocean, their massing bulk limning the horizon; now they fed in across the land in front of him, light falling through them in broken shafts, a reminder that the landscape was so immense the motion of entire weather systems was visible.

Half a century ago this region had been sustained by mines, vast operations serviced by teams of workers based in Perth and elsewhere who flew in and out on long rotations. But as the world's economies shuddered and cracked through the twenties and thirties, the demand for minerals dried up and one by one the mines closed. In places along the coast their remnants are still visible, vast machines and pits, rusting facilities hugging the bays, already half subsumed into the contours of the land.

That first day, he drove for four hours, the road unfurling hypnotically in front of him, the skeletal remains of the trees that dotted the valleys and declivities moving by in silence. Only when he turned onto the side road to the array did the land begin to rise, its undulations dotted here and there with low trees and broken reefs of rock until he reached the red earth of the plateau.

When he opened the gate he found himself staring out at the serried lines of white antenna dishes that made up the array spreading off into the distance. The day was almost windless, the space so quiet he could hear himself breathe. And for a second he felt himself give way to that silence, lost in something so much larger than himself it was impossible to comprehend.

5

The call from Adam comes late. Noah is at home alone, so absorbed in his work that for a second or two he considers not answering. When he picks up, Adam's face appears in one of his overlays.

'Noah?' he says. 'Are you at home? We need to talk.'

'About what?'

A moment passes. Then Adam says, 'It's your mother. She's alive.'

6

Noah is in the kitchen behind the control room when he receives an alert from the array's system. It is late, well after one, and the only people still in attendance are him and Jin. He calls up the data, assuming it will be another of the mildly anomalous signals they detect from time to time, his body tensing as it unfurls in his overlays, his preconscious brain recognising that the scattering of pulses is too structured to be natural before his conscious mind has fully comprehended what he is looking at.

'Where is it from?' he asks.

The system gives him the coordinates. Although he does not need to, Noah pulls up the reference, confirms his memory is correct. In Sagittarius, just south of the galactic equator.

His hand shaking he hurries back into the control room and pulls the data up on his screen. Represented graphically the signal is unmistakeable; at the sight of it he goes still inside. 'Sound on,' he says, and all at once the room fills with a shriek of what seems static or concentrated distortion, a long burst that continues for ten seconds, fifteen, before disappearing and beginning again.

'Is this live?' he asks, and the system tells him it is. 'Is it recording?' Again the system confirms it is. On the other side of the control room Jin has risen to his feet.

'Is that . . . ?' he asks, but Noah doesn't answer, just sits staring at his screen.

7

The sequence repeats itself twice more during the following minutes, three bursts of just over thirty seconds each, separated by roughly three seconds of silence; then, after the third sequence, it falls quiet.

Jin and Noah sit without speaking, alert in case it begins again. Only when it is finally clear that whatever it was has stopped does Jin break the silence.

'That *was* what it sounded like, wasn't it?'

Frightened that putting it into words will somehow dissipate what he has just heard, Noah struggles to form an answer. But eventually he nods. 'I don't know,' he says. 'Perhaps. I think so.'

Over the hours that follow they perform the tests necessary to eliminate false positives, repeating each of them twice, then a third time. With so much junk in orbit it is important to be certain that they have not merely picked up some malfunctioning piece of military hardware, or a terrestrial signal reflected back at them by a satellite. But each time the results are the same: the source of the transmission was not terrestrial or from an object in orbit. Instead its motion was consistent with the rotation of the Milky Way, meaning it emanated from somewhere outside the solar system.

As the transmission source begins to move towards the horizon, Jin seats himself next to Noah.

'We need to talk to the observatory at Karoo,' he says. 'If it recurs they'll be able to pick it up, confirm our results.'

Although Jin knows Naledi, the supervisor of the South Africa facility, better than Noah, they decide Noah should make the request. Calling up Karoo's details, he pings her to ask the observatory to scan the relevant patch of sky. Naledi pings them back almost immediately.

Need more information.

Anomalous intermittent radio source detected in Sagittarius, Noah replies. *Exhibiting sidereal motion.*

Pulsar? Potential supernova?

Not pulsar.

Then what?

Unclear. Coherent and repeating at 1420 MHz.

A moment later her face appears on the screen in front of Noah. 'Repeating how?' she asks without preliminaries.

'Three bursts 32.7 seconds in duration and 3.27 seconds apart. The entire sequence seems to have been repeated three times, with a gap between each sequence of 32.7 seconds.'

'You should have heard it,' says Jin, leaning in. 'Clear as day.'

Naledi looks away, absorbed in some mental calculation. Then she nods. 'Send me the data; we'll see what we can do. And Noah?'

'Yes?'

'I'll make sure we keep this to ourselves.'

Just before dawn, as the source of the signal passes below the horizon, Noah walks outside. It is cold, the desert air dry. To the east the approaching morning is pale pink, the sky above almost colourless. He knows – they all know – the significance of the signal's frequency, which sits in the band known as the hydrogen line, the clear spot in the electromagnetic spectrum at which a signal would suffer the least interference. Turning to the west he tries to pinpoint where the source of the signal must be by now, aware it will be in range of Karoo in an hour or two.

Looking down he realises his legs are shaking, that he is frightened not just because they might not find the signal again, or it might be dismissed as an anomaly, but because it might really be what it seems to be.

8

Noah first conceived the project a year after he started postdoctoral work. He had been involved in a program dedicated to sifting data from the old space telescopes for evidence of methane and other fingerprints of life, when he began to sketch out a proposal to use the array to search for signals from alien cultures.

It was not a new idea. For much of the second half of the twentieth century scientists around the world had cooperated on programs designed to scan the skies for alien transmissions, many of them believing it would be only a matter of time before evidence of other life and civilisations was found. But as the decades passed without results, that conviction began to wane. In the early years of the twenty-first century there was a brief renewal of interest, spurred by the suggestion that life might lurk in the oceans of the moons of Saturn and Jupiter, and by the discovery of planets around other stars.

But that interest didn't last. Faced with the escalating

environmental crisis and impoverished by debt and economic stagnation, governments began to cut back on investment in astronomy, diverting their resources to research into alternative energies and mitigation strategies. Amongst the first programs to be cut were those related to the hunt for alien intelligence. There was little reason to keep them: more than sixty years of searching had found no evidence at all, nothing, in fact, except silence.

Exactly why those searches failed was impossible to know. Perhaps life was rare, intelligence even more so. Perhaps humans arrived too late or too early and the heyday of galactic civilisation had already passed, or lay billions of years in the future. Perhaps the assumption that others would use radio to communicate had been mistaken, perhaps the search should have concentrated on laser signals, or neutrinos. Or perhaps it was simply that there was nobody out there to find.

The project Noah designed was an attempt to step past these failures and begin again. The first searches for signals had concentrated on scanning the entire sky in tiny sections, focusing on each part for a few seconds before moving on. The problem with this approach was that if the radio source was a beacon that sent a signal once an hour or once a day or once a year, it was highly unlikely to be detected. So in its place Noah proposed to direct a search into the galactic plane, where the stars are densest, and then to search each sector for as long as possible, using the computational power of the array's system to sift the data for anomalies.

His superiors regarded the project as quixotic and a waste of resources. And for the past four years his efforts have yielded nothing: no signals, no suggestion there is anything out there except emptiness. Until now.

9

As a child he was always afraid. Sound was too close, too huge. Things moved too fast. People came and went, looming into view and disappearing, their movements erratic, unpredictable, their voices a clamour of undifferentiated noise.

In his mind that time seems to stretch on and on. He has read enough about the science of memory, the way it encodes in the brain, to know he should have forgotten, but he hasn't; instead it remains vivid, unsettlingly near at hand.

He remembers the first time he stopped being frightened. He was with his therapist, Rayna – he recalls the office, the hum of the air-conditioning, the line of puzzles on the table. She had placed him in a plastic chair at the table and then sat opposite him. He was afraid – as he always was – but Rayna didn't try to touch him or talk to him.

Eventually he felt himself relax into the sense of calm Rayna and the office projected. Finally she took a breath and introduced herself. Usually when people spoke it was like cymbals clashing, but her voice was gentle, soothing.

'I don't need you to talk to me, Noah,' she said. 'I'm okay if we just sit here.'

She was looking past him, her attention focused somewhere just beyond him. And though he didn't understand it quite then, in that moment something unknotted inside him.

1 0

As Noah and Jin wait for Sagittarius to rise the following evening a hush falls over the control room. They have done their best to keep the circle of those who know about the signal small, but inevitably word has leaked out and several other technicians have gathered to wait with them.

Noah is tense, hyper-alert. He has not slept, does not think he could if he tried. During the afternoon he had gone back through the data, but after analysing and reanalysing the readings he is next to certain the signal emanated from a star five hundred light years away known only as SKA-2165. M-class, seven known exoplanets, two in the habitable zone.

Yet despite its strength and clarity the night before the signal has not been detected elsewhere. Late in the morning Naledi pinged them to say they had found no trace of it, and suggested they contact the Atacama array in Chile.

Noah was reluctant, uncomfortable with the idea of letting more of the astronomic community learn of the signal before they had more conclusive evidence. But at Jin's urging he acceded. The leader of the Chilean team was more sceptical than Naledi, and perhaps with good reason, for despite agreeing to concentrate on SKA-2165 they had detected nothing.

As Noah has reminded Jin a number of times, the failure of Karoo and Atacama to detect the signal is not necessarily significant. Noah's program was designed on the assumption that the power demands of broadcasting an omnidirectional signal are prohibitive, meaning any transmissions are more likely to be produced by beacons, either sweeping a single beam like a lighthouse or sending a rotating sequence of short signals to a series of specific targets. In both cases it was possible for hours or days or even longer to pass between each signal. This would explain why the signal had not been detected before now: nobody had looked at the right moment. But it also meant that waiting for it to recur might be a long process.

There is another possibility. If the signal really is a beacon it seems logical to Noah that it is designed to draw their attention, and that if they look more closely they will find another signal emanating from the same source, perhaps a longer signal with more information. And so while they wait for the signal to recur they will also look for that.

11

After that day with Rayna things were different. He wasn't just less frightened, he felt connected somehow, less lonely. It didn't happen all at once, of course, but he remembers a moment on the train, the colour of the light on a map of destinations, and somewhere in its warmth a sense of peace.

His mother did the best she could. Although there were no longer programs to help parents with children who needed therapy, she managed to find somebody locally who helped develop a set of exercises for him. Looking back he can see they were designed to help him with language by moulding his perceptual processes, to help him hear the way others did, but at the time he mostly enjoyed the calm he felt when he sat with Summer and worked through them. Although he loved her he was also afraid of her, of her frustration, but when they did the exercises she was always patient, always gentle.

He knows enough now about the science to understand the differences between his brain and those of most people. Where they think in language he thinks in image and symbol, where they think in social time he thinks in space and patterns. Yet he still finds it difficult to grasp the ease with which others seem to accommodate language, the way it supports them, sustains them: for him it has always been clumsy, artificial even.

By the time he was ready to start school he had some words, although not enough. And school terrified him, especially at first. The other children weren't cruel, but they were loud, baffling, unsettlingly erratic. Some days he barely spoke, just sat drawing diagrams or staring out the window. He had discovered astronomy by then, and when things became too much he would retreat, losing himself in calculations of the orbits of the planets, or by imagining he was out there, in the silence of the void. He can still remember the shape of the window in his first- and second-form classrooms, and the way the sky moved against the roofs in the streets on the walk home from school.

Yet he was still afraid so much of the time. Sometimes he would forget he was meant to stay home, and head out into the fields or down to the sheds to watch adults working. It was fascinating to him, the way they concentrated on their task. For a while after they moved to the country there was a man called Sean who built boats in his barn, beautiful craft that echoed the shape of the boats that had been used in the area thousands of years before. Noah watched the way the wood formed itself under his hands, the emergence of order. It was the plane he loved best, not the electric one but the handheld one, the way it moved with the grain, the wood curving up from its blade in long shavings. He found most smells overwhelming, disgusting, but the scent of the wood, its hot whiff of burning, was magical.

12

As the night wears on they grow restive, distracted by their failure to detect either the signal or some other transmission on another frequency. Worried that they have made a mistake, or the equipment is faulty in some way, Jin checks the systems over and over again, but finds nothing wrong.

Although Noah tries to disguise his anxiety he becomes steadily more agitated, the possibility that the result will not be repeatable, that it will turn out to have been nothing more than an anomaly, almost unbearable.

And so he tells himself it is just a matter of looking,

that they will find it again no matter what. The array is one of the most sensitive deep-space observation facilities on Earth, capable of picking up whispers from across the universe, its system powerful enough to sort through the extraordinary density of that information, to comb it for the tiniest details.

Sometimes he finds it dizzying, the thought of all that computer power, the depth to which they can probe. From here it has been possible to observe hundreds of billions of galaxies, to not just plot their positions but map their structure and movement, the shift and flow of galactic clusters and superclusters through the fabric of the universe.

13

In the days after Adam's call Noah walls himself off, refusing Adam and Ellie's repeated attempts to contact him. He knows they are concerned about him, are worried about his reaction, but he is not willing to discuss it.

The truth is they are unable to understand. He doesn't just not want to see her, he *can't* see her, can't bear being reminded of what happened. He's angry, he knows that, but he is also afraid, not just that she might hurt him again but that he might let her, that he might not be able to prevent himself from forgiving her. And so he throws himself into work, concentrating on the preparations for his coming trip to the array. Eventually Lijuan calls him, and after a short conversation tells him Adam is there with her, that he wants to speak to him.

He almost hangs up but before he can, Adam comes on the line.

'Noah,' he says. 'We've been trying to contact you. Are you okay? I understand if you're angry or frightened, but you need to see her.'

Noah stares ahead, willing the conversation to be over. 'No I don't.'

'Not for her sake, Noah, for yours. Before it's too late.'

His tone of voice makes Noah hesitate. 'What do you mean?'

Adam says, 'She's sick, Noah. Very sick.'

14

Near dawn, when the star sets, they ask the system to collate the data and share it with them, but no matter how many times they review it there is no sign of either a repeat signal or a second transmission. Despite his determination to stay calm Noah is perturbed, alarmed that the discovery is slipping away from him. It makes no sense: why send these squirts of random noise? Why not send something that can be recognised, audio or numbers, some kind of binary code? Why broadcast noise into space?

15

Although Adam and Ellie offer to accompany him he is determined to visit her on his own, picking a time he knows he will be undisturbed by other concerns. When the day arrives he walks the short distance from the train station to the hospital, rides the elevator up to her room. Outside her door he stops, almost turns and runs away, but then he steels himself and steps inside.

He does not recognise her at first. She is lying in the bed nearest the window, her once-blonde hair now grey, her face drawn. As he approaches she turns towards him.

'Noah,' she says.

He doesn't answer, cannot speak.

She pushes herself upright, her face tightening in pain. 'You came. I wasn't sure you would.'

When he still doesn't reply she gestures at the seat beside her bed. 'Please,' she says, 'sit down.'

He is trembling, unwilling to let her see his distress.

'Did your grandfather tell you to come?' Her face shows she knows the answer to that without him telling her. 'So you know . . .?'

Noah nods and she looks away for a minute. 'He said you're going away soon.'

'To Western Australia,' he says in a strangled voice. 'I have time on the array out there each year.'

'He says you're looking for alien life.'

'Not life. I'm looking for signs of intelligence.'

'You think it's there?'

'Perhaps.'

Her face softens. 'When you were a boy you were so fascinated by the stars. We had a telescope, do you remember? You were amazing. You learned the names of the constellations and the planets. Sometimes you would recite them.' She smiles, then catches herself. 'I'm sorry, it's not fair of me to talk like that.'

'It's okay,' he says, less stiffly.

For a long moment the two of them are quiet. Finally Summer asks, 'Are you happy? In your work? In your life?'

Uncertain of how to answer, he hesitates. 'I suppose,' he says at last. The feeling welling in his throat is choking him.

She closes her eyes. 'I'm glad,' she says. 'You know, I don't expect you to forgive me. It was wrong. I know that now, I knew it then. I told myself I was doing it for you, that it was better for you not to be with me, but really it was because I didn't know what to do, and I thought that by running away I could make everything stop, but I was wrong. I just made it all worse, so much worse.' She stops. 'I need you to know something, though. That it wasn't because I didn't love you – I did, so, so much. It's just that I was afraid.'

She turns on her side. 'I have something,' she says. 'Something I want you to have. Here, get me my bag.'

From her bedside cupboard he takes out her bag, which she opens with one hand. After a search she pulls forth a child's plastic toy, offers it to him.

Turning it over he recognises it as the Sixteenth Doctor, one of a collection he had as a child.

'Do you remember it?'

'I thought we lost them all.'

'I found it, later, in the bag I had. I must have put it there to keep it safe. We used to watch it together, remember?'

'He was my favourite.'

She laughs. 'Mine was the fourteenth, but that's because he was the first one I saw as a kid.'

He goes to hand the figure back but she lifts a hand to stop him.

'Keep it. It's yours.' She sits forward. 'Will you come again?' she asks.

'I don't know,' he says. 'I have to go away.'

'I understand,' she says.

1 6

By the end of the third night Jin and Noah are exhausted, dispirited. Despite repeated surveys of the area they have found no evidence of a second transmission, nor has the signal been repeated. When they contact Karoo, Naledi appears on their screen, telling them she's not confident they can devote more time to the search.

'I'm not saying we won't continue to look when we can,' she says. 'But for now we can't hold up our other work any longer.' She clears her throat. 'I don't want to be the one to say this, but have you considered the possibility that the first signal was a glitch of some sort? Or a natural phenomenon?'

'We've checked and double-checked for glitches,' Noah says. 'And its structure is too regular to be natural, you know that as well as I do.'

'Pulsars have structure.'

'Not like this,' he says.

'Then maybe it's not what we think it is,' Naledi says. 'Maybe it's not a beacon. Or if it is, maybe it's been running for so long that whoever set it up has forgotten about it, and whatever back end or second message it was supposed to point us to is no longer operational. Either way we don't know when the signal will recur and we can't keep looking endlessly until it does.'

Once she has gone Noah stands to leave.

'Do you think she's right?' Jin asks.

'No. It's a signal,' he says. 'It has to be. But there's something we're not seeing.'

17

In the weeks and months after she disappeared it was as if he was coming apart, dissolving. The first days were spent with Adam, in transit to a crisis centre. In the beginning they travelled in a truck, crowded in with dozens of others, bouncing and thumping against one another; later they walked, stumbling through the destruction left by the flood. Everywhere refuse lay tumbled against trees and buildings; it was filthy, stinking. They came across bodies, animals mostly – cows and sheep caught in the branches of trees, dogs and badgers lying by the side of the road – but also humans, usually in plastic body bags tagged and piled on street corners, but sometimes exposed to the elements or half buried in the wreckage.

Noah was only dimly aware of Adam walking beside him, of his hand around his own. When he grew weary Adam lifted him onto his shoulders, and although his proximity, the sharp smell of his hair and body, made Noah uncomfortable, he was too tired to resist.

It was several days before he realised Summer was really gone. They were in the relocation camp by then, sleeping on mattresses in a sports hall.

'When's my mum coming back?' he asked.

Adam fell still, one finger poised above his screen. Setting it down he came and sat next to Noah.

'I don't know,' he said. 'I've been trying to find her.'

'Can't you call her?'

Adam shook his head. 'She's not answering.'

'Perhaps she's lost her phone?'

'Perhaps,' Adam said quietly.

'Is she dead?' Noah asked then, the words seeming to come from far away.

'No,' Adam said. 'I don't think so.'

Looking back Noah wonders when it was that Adam himself truly understood Summer had left them. Was it that first day, when they looked for her so frantically, or later, at the crisis centre? Or back in London, as they squatted in Adam's hotel? Or was there no single moment when he knew, only a slow realisation seeping its way into his consciousness?

When they reached Australia it was like being five all over again, people and sounds and smells he did not recognise crowding in on him. It was so bright, so loud after the quiet of the fields. And through it all the absence of his mother like a hollow at the centre of him, the feeling so huge, so overwhelming, he was afraid to give into it.

18

Noah is alone in his room when the idea comes to him. For three days he has been listening to the signal over and over again. It is like an extended squawk, a cacophonous shriek that oscillates up and down, barely distinguishable from random noise. But as he directs the system to replay it to him yet again he suddenly recalls an article about research into the language of dolphins, the fact that the complex structure of the sounds they make only became apparent once their vocalisations were slowed down and reanalysed. A shiver running up his spine, he directs the system to slow the signal to one-hundredth of its current speed, and a moment later a sound fills the room.

At first he cannot fathom what he is hearing: it sounds like a Geiger counter, a series of clicks and whistles bouncing up and down in frequency, strange yet curiously beautiful, like whale song.

Legs shaking beneath him he runs to Jin's room, pounds on the door. The instant Jin opens it he barges in. As the recording plays he sees the emotions move across Jin's face, relief turning to amazement then exultation.

'What do you think it is?' Jin asks once it is finished.

'I don't know. Some kind of notation? Mathematics? A code?'

'Play it again,' Jin says. Noah directs the system and the wash of sound returns. But as it loops and overlays he remembers something else, and instructs the system to scan the signal. A moment later it returns a result.

'It's language,' he says.

'What?' Jin laughs, his face still alight.

'It's not maths or numbers or code, it's language.'

'Really? How do you know?'

'Language is like any information; even if you don't understand it, you can break it down into its component elements and graph the frequency of those elements, plot a line from the most frequent to the least. If it's just noise or babble, there'll be lots of sounds and they'll be distributed at random, so the line of the graph will be flat. But if it has structure, particular elements will recur more often than others, and the slope of the graph changes. It doesn't matter what the language is – English, Mandarin, Khmer – that slope is always the same, it's always -1.'

'So?' Jin says.

'It's the same with whales and dolphins. We can't understand them, but because we can map the structure of the sounds they make, and because the graph shows the same slope of -1, we know the sounds they're making are language.'

'So you're saying this . . . this sound . . . produces that same result?'

'Exactly.'

'But why?' Jin asks. 'Why send us something we can't understand? And what are they saying?'

1 9

It cannot be kept secret, of course. Nothing is ever secret for long, not any more. And so after discussions with the team it is decided to release the news in advance of publication. Jin is excited about this; it will mean fame for them. There is some difficulty to be negotiated around who will announce it, whether the honour should be handed to a politician or one of the international authorities, but in the end they defer to the protocols laid down a century before, agreeing that since it is a scientific matter, it should fall to Noah to make the announcement.

Noah keeps his distance from the political arguments, but the idea of getting up in front of the cameras terrifies him, although not as much as the thought of all the questions, everybody expecting him to answer them, wanting a piece of him.

20

As a child he spent many nights out in the garden of whichever house his mother was living in, looking at the stars with the telescope she'd bought him. They seemed so perfect, so still, their beauty disguising their unimaginable violence, the cataclysm of their birth and death. It was possible to be afraid of that but he was not; instead it seemed wondrous such violence could create such beauty, that the fragrant garden in which he stood, the fragile web of life around him, was tumbling through the vastness of space. Those gardens, those houses, the land that surrounded them are gone now, vanished beneath the sea, yet they still exist somewhere, in some possible world. As a scientist he knows that experience of time is an illusion, that all times exist equally, all possible worlds are present in every moment. That in another universe those gardens are still there, he is still there, that the past never ended.

21

On his last night at the array they hold a party for him and Jin, the technicians and the few postgraduates gathering in the rec room. There is music and dancing, and toasts to the two of them, a sense of shared excitement, but Noah, still exercised by the question of the signal and what it might mean, wanders out to stand in the desert under the stars.

The next morning he leaves early, heading west towards the ocean. Jin is to follow later. It has grown cooler overnight, a storm system feeding down from the north. Arranging his flight, he watched satellite images of it, the great bands of cloud and moisture, and was reminded of the way the land is never still, existing instead in a process of constant change: the movement of the weather, the march of the seasons, the long oscillation of climate systems, their cycles repeated over and over.

Outside, the desert moves by. The first time he came here the sheer emptiness of the landscape frightened him, but as the years have passed he has learned to appreciate the echoes of other ages contained within it, to love the frozen archaeology of the broken rock, the lifted plains, the dust. Now when he looks out at the desert he sees what he sees in the sky, the great depth of time, and silence.

2 2

The constellations have names they have borne for millennia. Each one a deep well of memory. The seven sisters, the dog, the hunter – these names recur in cultures across the world, suggesting they share a common ancestor, that the first humans bore them with them out of Africa.

It is remarkable to Noah that language should persist in this way, that it should have these deep origins: to him it has always seemed atomised, arbitrary, a collection of sounds the meanings of which might as well be accidental. But in reality it connects him, connects everybody, not just to each other but to the distant past.

Yet what of the future? What will be here eons from now? The ice is almost gone, but while it may take millions of years, there is little doubt that one day it will return, creeping back to cover the land, and the world will change once more, the turmoil and destruction of the past century being little more than a spasm, an interregnum in the great cycles of the planet's existence. Perhaps there will still be humans then, men and women as different from him as he is from those ancient people on the plains of Africa; perhaps some of them will have spread outward, to the stars, borne there in great ships just as boats bore the first humans across Earth's oceans. Either way they will carry within them the memory of this time, this past, like a stone borne in the mouth, just as he bears the memory of those ancient travellers in him.

23

He was not sure he would come until he was almost there, but now that he stands at the door he understands why he needed to.

She is lying on her back, her mouth open, her face so thin he thinks for a second she is dead. But then she takes a breath, the slow, shuddering sound startling him.

Drawing out a chair he sits. He had thought they might speak, that there might be things they could say to each other, the things left unsaid last time he came, but seeing her he knows that will not happen.

Remembering what people have said about voices, and the capacity for someone to hear even when seemingly unconscious, he knows he must speak, but he cannot decide what to say. Then he recalls Adam urging him not to be afraid, to just say anything, that it is the sound of his voice that matters, her knowing he is there. So he begins to talk to her about the project, about why he has been away. He tells her about the signal, about trying to decipher it, about all his time out in the desert.

'We've found something,' he says. 'Something important. We don't know what it is, what it's saying, only that it's artificial, that somebody is sending it.'

And as he speaks he suddenly understands. They have

been worrying about what the signal says, what it means, but that's not the point. Whoever they are, whatever they are, they have not chosen the language of numbers or mathematics, they have chosen words, and not in order to be understood, but merely to speak. Noah thinks they must be beings who are aware that what is said is less important than the act of speaking, letting people know they are there. Because whatever else it may say, the message says that. We are here. You are not alone.

Hello.

24

It is crowded in the conference room, media reps pushing this way and that. Panic gripping him, Noah wills himself to be calm. At the back of the room he sees Adam with Lijuan; beside them Ellie is talking to Amir and Lijuan's husband, Dylan. His grandfather lifts a hand in greeting, but before Noah can respond the media officer who has been looking after him touches his arm and says in a whisper it is good there are so many here, that this means they know something big is up. But he cannot listen, cannot think. In front of him a woman appears, speaking to Jin but looking at him. One of the journalists, he realises.

'This is Noah, is it?' she asks, and the media officer smiles and tells her it is.

'It's all very mysterious,' she says, 'an astronomer in a global media conference.'

He opens his mouth to make an excuse, but before he can Jin is there, pulling him aside. Gratefully Noah lets him shuffle him away, out into the corridor.

'Thank you,' he says once they are clear of the crowd.

'You didn't look like you were enjoying yourself,' Jin laughs. Reaching up he straightens Noah's collar. 'It'll be okay, you know. You don't have to say much.'

'I know,' Noah says. Further along the corridor he sees a door. Gesturing toward it he says, 'I just need to be alone for a moment.'

Outside it is cooler, the stars unusually bright. Across the road, through the trees, he can see the lights of the city; closer in bats chitter and brawl in the foliage.

Behind the scenes the debate has already begun about how to respond to the signal. Although most of them are eager to send a reply, some of his colleagues are already anticipating public anxiety about attracting the attention of other species. Yet nobody seriously believes there will not be a response of some sort: once the location of the signal's source is made public people all over the world will want to send signals of their own.

It is not a debate they need to resolve quickly, of course. Even once they do respond, it will be five hundred years before the message reaches SKA-2165, another five hundred before anyone hears back. He will be gone by then, as will Adam, Ellie, Lijuan, Dylan, Jin, Amir, all of them vanished into the distant past, their passage through the world remembered, if at all, by a handful of video recordings, a scattering of data traces.

Who will be here to receive the reply when it comes? What kind of world will they inhabit? Sometimes it is difficult for Noah to believe humanity will survive at all, so violent have the planet's convulsions become. To the north the ice is gone, the Arctic a gleaming hump of water; to the south the Antarctic ice sheet is collapsing, faster every year; in South America the Amazon is burning. The planet's crust is shifting, buckling and cracking as the weight of the ice recedes.

Behind him he hears Jin's voice telling him it is time. Opening his hand he looks down at the figure, its features nearly rubbed away by the passage of time. And as he does he remembers, or thinks he does. Overhead the sky so deep he might fall, tumble upwards, lose himself in that immensity. The feeling like vertigo.

Like flight.

THE
SHIMMER

It is Bo's idea they go down to the water, just the four of them, join one of the parties out on the islands to celebrate Izzie's birthday. Malla and Nam had other plans, Nam particularly, but when Bo suggests it Izzie knows immediately it is what she wants to do.

They ride the train as far as it will take them, crammed into the carriage with a handful of others bound for the party and with the last commuters, then they pile out onto the station. It is a warm night, the train lines throwing sparks in the darkness, and as they make their way down the stairs Bo loops his arm around her neck and leans in towards her. For the past few weeks he has been working on a reconstruction project, and although he has showered the smell of dust and solvents still lingers on his skin. She doesn't care; she loves the way he smells, loves the strength of his arms, his easy manner.

Malla and Nam like him as well, although Izzie knows both of them are sometimes a little wary of him: in contrast to the three of them he was raised on a co-op, and as with a lot of people brought up like that he grew a little feral, his time spent working in the gardens or messing about with the other kids, meaning he has little interest in the hothouse world inhabited by Malla and Nam and, to a lesser extent, Izzie.

When they met it was exactly this that drew her to him: unlike most of her friends he had a reassuring solidity, a sense of who he was that was not hostage to what others thought of him. She knew even then that they were not suited in any long-term way, that the things she cares about are not the things he cares about, and so although he is attentive when she does, she tends not to speak about her plans for the future. Yet as the months have passed she has begun to feel guilty about this holding back, guilty she might be using him, because as much as she loves him now she knows this is not forever, that she will move on and leave him.

At the exit from the station they turn left along the floating duckboard connecting it to the jetty. Before the sea rose this place was a suburb, now it is part of the Floodline, a watery graveyard of partly submerged streets and buildings sprawling half a kilometre inland along much of the city's fringe. Where the apartments rise above the water people can be seen on balconies or moving about indoors, their voices raised in Bengali and Malayalam, Chinese and English. From some music can be heard, or laughter; in others people sit staring out, fanning themselves or drinking.

As they reach the jetty Nam and Malla take Izzie by the arm and pull her after them, laughing and shouting. Aware that Bo sometimes finds the pair's giddiness irritating she glances back, but he only whoops and chases after her, and in a moment they are all running, racing each other on and out.

At the jetty's end a small crowd has gathered, waiting for the boats that will bear them to the island. As the four of them come sprinting in several people turn and greet them, eyes alight.

Weaving his way to the front Nam calls out to one of the boats, beckoning it towards him, but the young woman steering it tells him he has to wait in line. He darts back and grabs Izzie by the arm, dragging her forward. 'Can't you make an exception?' he says. 'It's my friend's birthday.'

Izzie pulls away, lifting a hand to dismiss Nam's suggestion, but the woman sculls the boat in closer.

'Really?' she says.

'Would I lie to you?' Nam asks, assuming a pose of teasing disbelief.

The woman in the boat laughs. 'I don't know. What do the other people waiting think?'

Several of them pat Izzie on the shoulder, urging her to take the boat. Embarrassed she steps back, shaking her head, but they push her forward again, and so, relenting, she lets Nam take her hand and conduct her and Malla and finally Bo into the boat.

Out on the water voices and laughter are audible, drifting across from the island; occasionally somebody shouts, or there is a shriek as people stumble into the water. The party tonight is nominally for the solstice, although the collectives that organise these Floodline parties throw them for the full moon and the equinox, and any of a dozen other reasons as well. Yet as the boat slips across the dark water there does seem something oddly perfect about tonight, the soft warmth and stillness of the air. Where the prow cuts the water it peels back, luminescent plankton flaring blue and green within it. It is magical, yet watching, Izzie remembers reading somewhere that the light is only released as the plankton die, its beauty really the snuffing out of a million tiny lives.

From the front of the boat Malla calls out to her. Moving carefully so as not to overbalance the craft Izzie crawls forward and Malla points down into the water, where glowing fish dart and turn like stars beneath the surface.

Izzie gasps, and behind her the woman steering the boat laughs. 'They're gengineered,' she says. 'Somebody released them a few years ago and they seem to have survived in the wild. You're lucky – we don't see them every night.'

'They must be here for your birthday, Iz,' Malla says with a grin; reaching down, Izzie flicks a handful of water up at her. Malla squeals and twists away, the boat rocking beneath them, ripples of phosphor spreading away from it.

And then they are on the shore, scrambling out of the boat and onto the beach. The island is tidal, a patch of sand gathered around a line of submerged buildings, but at its highest point low trees grow, dark against the pale sand, and in front of them a crowd is already gathered, dancing and talking.

'Come on,' Malla says, and they head off along the beach towards the voices.

As they draw closer their lenses and aural receptors interface with the party, the ecstatic beat of the music filling their heads and the virtual environment dropping into their overlays, enveloping them. Izzie gasps, delighted: although she has been to a few of these parties she is always amazed by what the collectives do for them. Now temple walls rise up, lit by Chinese lanterns; in the space overhead dragons swoop and turn, their paths criss-crossed by birds and other magical creatures.

Whooping, Nam throws his arms up in the air and twirls around, his street clothes disappearing, replaced in her overlays by one of his virtual creations, gorgeous feathered wings sprouting from his back, ribbons of light trailing from his hands and feet. Catching Izzie's eye he grabs her hands and spins her across to Bo, who pulls her close, pressing his lips to hers until Malla appears and drags her into the crowd.

She is not sure how long they dance – an hour, maybe two – looping and twining themselves around others, all of them lost in the music, the lights, the sweaty press of their bodies. She dances with Malla and Nam, later with Bo, then with a group of girls wearing shimmering masks. Eventually she notices a call from her mother flash up in her overlays. At first she ignores it, but then, realising how late it is, she pushes her way to the edge of the crowd and accepts the call.

'Hey, Mum,' she says. 'What's up?'

'Noah called,' says Lijuan. 'It's Adam.'

She falters. 'What about him?' she asks, although in the moment it takes her mother to reply she already knows.

'He's dead, sweetie,' Lijuan says.

'When?' she asks stupidly. Although they were not related by blood, Adam is the closest thing she has ever had to a grandparent.

'Earlier tonight. They think it was a heart attack.'

'Was Noah there?'

'At the end he was.'

'And you?'

'No, we only just found out.'

'I'm sorry,' she says numbly. 'Is Dad with you?'

Lijuan tells her he is.

'Do you want me to come home?'

'No,' Lijuan says. 'But I wanted you to hear it from me before you heard it somewhere else.'

Thanking her mother Izzie hangs up and turns back to the crowd spread across the sand behind her. A little way in she can see Malla, swaying with her head thrown back; beside her Bo is entwined with the girl the two of them were dancing with a moment before, motes of virtual light swirling around them.

Suddenly wanting to be rid of it all she switches off her overlays, the temples and swooping dragons and floating lanterns vanishing to reveal several hundred people moving in synch to music nobody but they can hear.

It is not the first time she has watched this sort of event

without overlays, but as always it makes the pleasure of the hours before seem trivial, absurd, so taking a step back she turns and follows the line of the beach out towards the point. It is quieter here, and lowering herself to the sand she sits and looks up to see there is colour in the sky, sheets and twisting skeins of green and blue and violet shifting and flowing against the darkness.

Lying back, she spreads her arms out at her side and stares up, trying to lose herself in the flickering dance of the lights, their constantly changing hue.

They have a proper name, of course, but most people call them the Shimmer. Nobody knows what is causing them: the best guess of most scientists is that they're related to a new instability in the Earth's magnetic fields, an instability that may presage the poles flipping from north to south, as they have occasionally in the distant past, although why that should be happening now is unclear. Some argue that it is a natural phenomenon. But there are also those who believe the process has been hastened by the events of the last century, claiming that the incremental changes to the Earth's rotation caused by the melting of the ice and the shifting of the crust as it adapted to its loss have destabilised the fields in new and unpredictable ways.

As Izzie lies there it is not these questions that concern

her, but the lights themselves, and the fact of Adam's death. It seems difficult to comprehend that the man she has known since she was a child could be gone.

He is only one of many, of course, just as she is, just as they all are, part of a movement in time, a river flowing ever on, bearing them away from the past. They have lost so much: Shanghai and Venice, Bangladesh, all those millions of lives.

Yet looking up, all of that seems to fall away, lost to the soundless dance of the Shimmer, the swirling shift and flare of its motion. She has seen footage of satellites moving through the aurora, the way it breaks across them like water, rolling on and over, and as she watches the waves of light she can feel herself moving with them, lifted up and on into a future that may be wonderful or terrible or a thousand things in between. And she realises that whatever else happens, this is not an end but a beginning.

It is always a beginning.

ACKNOWLEDGEMENTS

I am extremely grateful to the many people who helped create the book you are holding in your hand. My particular thanks to Neil Ballard for his assistance with various medical matters; Nigel Beebe, Ashley Hay and Stefan Keller for their input on some of the scientific material; and to Chris Flynn, Simon Ings, Pam Newton, Cat Sparks, Jonathan Strahan and Kirsten Tranter for their generosity in reading and responding to various drafts. I also owe a special debt of gratitude to my friends Kathryn Heyman, Garth Nix and Sean Williams, who helped me see the project for what it was at a difficult moment; my agent, David Miller; and Ben Ball, Meredith Rose and the rest of the team at Penguin for their enthusiasm and care in guiding the book to completion. And finally, and perhaps most importantly, my partner, Mardi McConnochie. This book would not have been possible without her love and

support, and that of my daughters, Annabelle and Lila:
I hope it repays their trust.

The quote on page 20 is from 'Human Moments in World War
III' by Don DeLillo, reprinted in *The Angel Esmeralda: Nine Stories*
(Picador).

ABOUT THE AUTHOR

James Bradley is a novelist and critic. His books include the novels *Wrack*, *The Deep Field* and *The Resurrectionist*, all of which won or were shortlisted for major Australian and international literary awards, a book of poetry, *Paper Nautilus*, *The Penguin Book of the Ocean*, and, most recently, a young adult science fiction novel, *The Silent Invasion*. As well as writing fiction, James writes and reviews for numerous Australian and international newspapers and magazines. Publications in which his work has appeared include *The Times Literary Supplement*, *The Guardian*, *The Washington Post*, *The Australian Literary Review*, *Australian Book Review*, *The Monthly* and *Locus*. In 2012 he was awarded the Pascall Prize for Australia's Critic of the Year. He blogs at cityoftongues.com.

James lives in Sydney, Australia.

For more fantastic fiction, author events, competitions,
limited editions and more

VISIT OUR WEBSITE
titanbooks.com

LIKE US ON FACEBOOK
facebook.com/titanbooks

FOLLOW US ON TWITTER
@TitanBooks

EMAIL US
readerfeedback@titanemail.com